WISE WORDS

WISE WORDS

Family Stories
That Bring the Proverbs to Life

Peter Leithart

LEGACY COMMUNICATIONS
Franklin, Tennessee

Co-published by Legacy Communications, Franklin, Tennessee, and
Great Christian Books, Elkton, Maryland.

ISBN   1-880692-23-6

To Noel
"An excellent wife, who can find?
For her worth is far above jewels."

CONTENTS

A NOTE TO PARENTS: DON'T READ THIS UNLESS YOU MUST

Writing a preface is the literary equivalent of parental doting. New parents assume their obsession with their own child is universally shared. To the enormous irritation of everyone else, they—or rather, we—exult in every colicky grimace, interpret every incoherent coo as a portent of eloquence, analyze every awkward kick and twist to calculate the chances of a future Olympic medal—all as if to say, "Look what we did! Look what we did!" Unfortunately, writers are vulnerable to the same vice. The following pages are written with the bold assumption that you are as interested in how this book came to be written as I am in telling you.

My intention in *Wise Words* was to write stories that would appeal to children as stories; that would challenge parents who read to their children; that would illustrate biblical Proverbs; and that would borrow imagery, plots, characters, settings, and themes from the Bible. Whether my stories appeal to children—other than my own, of course, who are deeply prejudiced—or challenge adults is, I suppose, for children and adults to judge.

At considerable risk of sounding pretentious, however, I will say a few words about my other goals. I hesitate to expose the foundations on which these stories are built. Every enterprise functions best when there is a division of labor; in literature, it is the reader's job to discover, not the author's. Besides, exposing foundations can cause stories to come crashing down. Given the likelihood that my point may be obscure, I reluctantly offer some guidelines for reading *Wise Words*. If you are the type of reader who does not want someone else to do your work for you, you have my permission to stop reading here and skip to the first story.

I am, by both temperament and training, a theologian rather than a storyteller, and my aim in writing these stories was as much theological as literary. Explaining that assertion requires a brief digression. In the Grimm brothers' story, "The Goose-Girl," a maidservant forces her mistress to change places with her, and the maid marries the prince herself. In the course of the story, the old king has occasion to ask the maid what punishment would be appropriate for a maid who takes her mistress's place and marries her mistress's fiance, and the girl replies ingenuously, "She deserves nothing better than to be stripped naked and put in a barrel that is studded with sharp nails, and two white horses should be harnessed to it to drag her up and down the street to her death." Unsurprisingly, the king answers, "That woman is you, and you have pronounced your own punishment."*

For myself, the maid's extraordinary combination of stupefying dullness and an impressive talent for designing pun-

---

* See Max Luthi, *The European Folktale: Form and Nature.* (Bloomington, IN: Indiana University Press, 1982), pp. 45-46.

ishments is not the most striking thing about this scene. Rather, this scene, repeated in other folk tales, is remarkably similar to Nathan's confrontation of David in 2 Samuel 12. Of course, Nathan had the sense to veil his meaning until the appropriate moment. Still, the parallel between the biblical event and the folk literary theme is undeniable.

Nor is this the only literary feature common to Scripture and folk tales. When three brothers are introduced at the beginning of a story, anyone with even minimal exposure to literature knows that the youngest one, no matter how oafish he initially appears, will turn out to be the most clever of all. Replacement of the heir by a younger brother is a common theme in Scripture as well, in Genesis particularly. The Grimm brothers' version of Cinderella ends with doves poking out the eyes of the two evil sisters (see Prov. 30:17). Folk heroes commonly battle dragons and just as commonly kill them with blows to the head (see Gen. 3:15). Having destroyed the dragon, the hero rescues a beautiful maiden (see Rev. 12). The Greek story of Donta recalls the exploits of Samson. Donta, a great warrior, possesses the rare ability to produce fighting men by clicking his teeth together. After one unsuccessful attempt, a beautiful princess extracts the secret of Donta's power, which she promptly relays to Donta's enemies.*

Whether or not direct connections between folk literature and Scriptural events exist we will never know. When I first noticed these analogies, I thought it might be intriguing to attempt some stories that would self-consciously employ biblical narrative techniques and themes. Such stories would, I hoped, be entertaining and might even illuminate the Bible.

---

* See Luthi, *The European Folktale*; *Once Upon a Time: On the Nature of Fairy Tales* (Bloomington, IN: Indiana University Press, 1976).

The Bible forms the background to *Wise Words* in two ways. First, this collection constitutes, in my own mind at least, an imaginative commentary on the book of Proverbs. In general, *Wise Words* follows what I have elsewhere called "the dramatic structure of Proverbs."* In the first eight chapters of Proverbs, two women are presented: Dame Folly and Lady Wisdom. The Prince, Solomon's son, must decide which he will embrace as his bride. At the end of the book, we learn that the Prince has resisted the temptations of Dame Folly. Proverbs 31 describes the superhuman labors of the "excellent wife," and we know the Prince has chosen well, for he has made Lady Wisdom his queen. *Wise Words* is constructed according to this blueprint.

Second, each story draws on Biblical stories and themes to illustrate the proverb that serves as its moral. Within these pages you will find a number of Biblical characters, including Adam and Eve (several times), Jacob and Esau, Nebuchadnezzar, a kind of reverse Joseph, David, Ezekiel, and others. The church appears in various guises, as she does in Scripture. Plots hinge on deaths and resurrections, rescues and battles, baptisms and ascensions of various sorts. Commands, when transgressed, have appropriately deadly consequences. Gardens, feasts, throne rooms, deserts, and mountains—all archetypal settings in Scripture—form the landscape in which the characters live and move and have their being.

Most of the stories splice together pieces of various biblical events into one narrative. Esau at a certain point turns into Nebuchadnezzar, Jacob into David, and always the First and Last Adams are lurking just beneath the surface. These last are by far the most prominent characters in my collec-

---

* *Biblical Horizons*, No. 43, November 1992. Available from Biblical Horizons, P.O. Box 1096, Niceville, Florida, 32588-1096.

tion, since Adam was the prototypical fool while Jesus is the Wisdom of God. Interweaving and overlapping of characters and plots occurs within Scripture itself, where Esau the hunter reminds us of Nimrod, the men of Gibeah act like Sodomites, Saul at first lives like Gideon but dies like Abimelech, David wanders in the wilderness like Israel, and Elijah, like Moses, flees to the Mount of the Lord to meet with God.

A more extended illustration of my method may help you better understand how these stories are constructed. "King Jacob of the Green Garland" is, at a basic level, a straightforward illustration of its moral. Eric's throne is insecure because of his injustice and cruelty, while Jacob's is established by the kindness and love he shows to his subjects. The plot weaves together threads from a number of Biblical events. Eric is an Adam, who because of pride loses his throne and must flee from his garden into the wilderness. Eric is "the Red" because he is like Esau, who despised his birthright and persecuted his righteous brother. Similarly, the real Esau was an Adam who sold his inheritance for food.

After his fall, Eric becomes, like Nebuchadnezzar, a beast in the wilderness. As Eric dies, he acknowledges his sins, and passes the kingship to his brother Jacob, the faithful heir. The king dies, but a new king rises to take his place. Jacob is the type of the Last Adam, who wins the throne, returns to his garden, and gives gifts to men. Later, he delivers the final blow to his enemy, William the Black, and thereafter rules his kingdom forever. The green garland crown signifies wisdom and justice (Proverbs 4:9); Jacob has become a tree of life to his people.

Perhaps I am plagued with the typical writer's disease of "reading too much into things." Perhaps I have even read too much into my own stories, though I do not think so. If, after reading my doting preface, your enthusiasm for the actual stories has waned, well, at least I warned you. I will not blame you if you are less impressed with my children than I am. This preface is offered with the hope that these comments will deepen your appreciation for my stories, and if they bring both pleasure and illumination to you and your children, I will be satisfied I have achieved my primary objective.

ACKNOWLEDGMENTS

everal years ago, desperate for paid writing assignments, I sent a draft of "The Three Princes" to George Grant, then of Coral Ridge Ministries, who received it with his usual enthusiasm. In a fit of irresponsible *hubris,* I said I could produce a couple dozen similar stories, and thus my doom was sealed. George's excitement for *Wise Words* continued even when mine dwindled, and for that, as well as for his support in getting it published, I am grateful.

Thanks to David Dunham, my publisher at Legacy, whose encouragement has been much needed and greatly appreciated.

My children—Woelke, Lindsey, Jordan, Sheffield, Christian, James, and Emma—formed the original audience for these stories and remain my most insightful and valued critics.

To my wife, Noel, I owe more than I can say. Were it not for her selfless willingness to take up my considerable and ever-growing slack, I would never have had the time or energy to complete these stories. She is truly an excellent wife, far more precious than rubies. This book is dedicated to her, with love.

Chapter I

ThE ThREE PRINCES

nce upon a time, there was a king who had three sons. Their names were Alexander, Julius, and Joseph. The king's name, of course, was Lothar.

King Lothar lived with his wife, Queen Emma, and his sons in a white castle on top of the highest mountain in that part of the world. From the west tower of the castle Lothar could view his entire kingdom, something he often did after supper in the cool quiet of twilight. His kingdom was as peaceful as the evening, and his people were rich and happy. King Lothar was happy too.

But Lothar had a problem. He was getting old, and he could not decide which of his sons should become king after him. In many kingdoms, this would not be a problem at all, because the oldest son takes the throne when his father dies. In Lothar's kingdom, though, the custom was different. The reigning king was allowed to give the crown to any son he wished.

Alexander was the oldest of Lothar's three sons. Alexander was the most handsome and graceful man in the whole kingdom, sleek as a leopard. When he was very small, he liked to climb onto his father's throne. He would put the crown on his head and gaze at himself in a mirror for

1

hours. When he danced at the royal balls, everyone stared in amazement.

Many of the people wanted Alexander to be king. Visitors would come from all over the world, they thought, just to see the handsome King Alexander. And their kingdom would be known from one end of the earth to the other.

Julius was next oldest, and he was the strongest man in the kingdom. When he entered battle, Julius seemed transformed from a man into a terrifying beast that crushed and trampled his enemies. Julius did not want to rule only the small kingdom of his father. He wanted to conquer other lands. Deep down, his desire was to rule the world.

Many people hoped Julius would be king. He would protect them from their enemies, they thought. And they were sure he could make their small kingdom into a great empire, maybe even the greatest in the world.

Joseph was the youngest. He was neither especially handsome nor especially strong. He spent most days taking care of his father's sheep and goats in the hills around the castle. Instead of going with Julius to battle in the springtime, Joseph would stay home to help the farmers plant their fields. Instead of spending winter dancing at the royal balls, as Alexander did, Joseph helped repair homes or dig animals out of snowdrifts.

No one could remember whether or not Joseph had ever been in a battle or if he had ever fought with anyone. Most of the people of the land thought Joseph would look pretty silly wearing a crown. No one thought Joseph would make a very good king—no one, that is, except Queen Emma. Joseph was her favorite. She wanted him to be king, and she told Lothar so day and night.

2

Lothar wanted Alexander to become king, but Alexander was rather proud. Julius made a good warrior, but Lothar was not sure he was smart enough to be a good king. But Joseph? Not Joseph, Lothar thought. Still, Lothar did not want to make Emma unhappy. So, he kept putting things off—unsure, as even kings sometimes are, about how he could please everyone and hoping somehow things would just work out.

Lothar's problem was solved by his old friend, Alfred. "Why don't you have a contest?" Alfred asked late one afternoon between mouthfuls of cheese and bread.

"Yes, yes." King Lothar was so excited he almost tipped over his wine. "We could assemble all the young maidens of the kingdom. They would choose the next king."

"But then Alexander would be sure to win," Alfred replied, glaring at Lothar. "No, no, Your Highness. If you let the maidens of the kingdom choose the next king, everyone will know you arranged for Alexander to be king. You must think of a fair contest, one that each of your sons will have a chance to win."

Lothar and Alfred fell silent. A moment later, a toothless smile spread across Alfred's wrinkled face. "I've got it! We could have them race. Yes! That would be an excellent contest. They could run around the castle three times, swim the moat, and then climb the wall to the west tower. The winner would be king."

Lothar's face turned as red as his beard. "You always did want Julius to be king, didn't you!"

"Sire, I . . ." Alfred stopped. He knew King Lothar was right. Julius would certainly win any contest of strength. A race would not be a fair contest.

Lothar and Alfred spent the rest of that afternoon and most of that night eating and drinking and trying to think of a fair contest for the three princes. By the time the sun rose the next morning, they had at last settled on a plan.

Later that very day, King Lothar called the gentlemen and ladies to his castle to hear his announcement. The three princes stood in the center of the great hall, dressed in their finest clothes.

King Lothar rose from his throne and began to speak. "As you all know, I must choose who shall become king when I die. This is a most important decision. If I select the right man, the kingdom will remain strong and rich and happy. If I make a bad choice, the kingdom will be doomed to weakness and misery.

"Alfred and I have decided that a contest will determine who will be king. The contest is this: Each of my sons will search for the most wonderful, most royal creature in the world. It must be a creature that represents what it means to be a king, and one that will be most useful to a king. I and twelve of the gentlemen of the kingdom will judge who has found the most wonderful and royal creature."

So the next day, Alexander, Julius, and Joseph set off to find the most wonderful creature in the world.

A month later, Alexander returned. The lords and ladies of the kingdom assembled before Lothar's throne in the great hall to find out what Alexander had brought with him. When all was quiet, Alexander clapped his hands, and two servants carried in a cage, covered with a golden cloth.

Alexander began to speak. "I have travelled many miles this past month. I travelled east to Asia, and there I found the most beautiful and royal creature in the world. See for yourselves its magnificent glory."

4

With that, Alexander pulled away the golden cloth. Inside the cage was a large peacock. The lords and ladies gasped. Several ladies screamed. One fainted out of wonder. It truly was the most beautiful creature they had ever seen. Its breast was deep blue like the evening sky. Its tail was covered with bright yellow eyes. It seemed to be wearing a delicate jewelled crown.

Alexander let the peacock out of its cage. It strutted about the great hall and screeched so loudly that everyone clapped his hands to his ears.

"With this creature at my side," Alexander said, "I will become the greatest king in the world. I will make the whole kingdom as beautiful as this peacock. Kings will come from over the Southern Sea to see my beautiful bird and my beautiful kingdom. The peacock will be the symbol of my rule."

King Lothar and the twelve gentlemen agreed that Alexander had found a wonderful and royal creature indeed. "But we must wait for the others," Lothar said.

At the end of the second month, Julius returned. The next morning, the lords and ladies gathered in the great hall to find out what Julius had brought back with him.

Julius swaggered into the room with his head high. He raised his hand to quiet the people and then began to speak in a loud voice. "I travelled many miles in these two months. I walked through deserts and jungles. I sailed across oceans. I went south to Africa, and there I found the most powerful and royal creature in the world."

Julius clapped his hands, and a servant entered the room, leading a great lion on a strong rope. The lion roared so loudly that the walls of the great hall shook. The lords and ladies were amazed. Several of the ladies screamed. One fainted out of fear.

5

"You are right to be afraid," Julius said. "He is strong and fierce. With this lion at my side, I will become the most feared king on earth. I will hunt and tear my enemies as a lion does its prey. This lion will be the symbol of my rule."

While he was still speaking, Alexander's peacock strutted into the room. The lion crouched staring at the peacock and then slowly circled it. Then the lion leaped at the peacock and ate it in one bite.

The lords and ladies were silent. The lion roared again. Surely Julius had found the more wonderful and royal creature. King Lothar and the twelve gentlemen were very pleased. "But we must wait for Joseph," Lothar said.

The next month seemed to take forever, as everyone waited and waited for Joseph to return. In every shop, around every dinner table, at every street corner, they talked of nothing but the princes' contest.

The people of the kingdom were certain that Julius would win. How could Joseph possibly find a more wonderful and royal creature than Julius's great lion? The butcher told the milkmaid Joseph would probably bring a lamb, which would make a nice snack for Julius's lion. Soon everyone was telling the butcher's joke. When Queen Emma heard it, though, she didn't laugh.

Finally, at the end of the third month, Joseph returned. With great excitement, the lords and ladies gathered before Lothar's throne in the great hall. The common people gathered outside straining to see and hear what would happen.

Joseph entered, wearing a dusty shepherd's cloak. He waited for the people to quiet, and then he began to speak. "I have not spent the past three months travelling. I went just over the mountain, to a place I had often been before. From

6

there I brought back the most wise and royal creature in the world."

Joseph disappeared into the crowd, and when he returned he was leading a pretty young girl by the hand. Like Joseph, she was dressed in a simple shepherd's cloak. The lords and ladies gasped. Several ladies screamed. One fainted out of disappointment. Before his mother could cover his mouth, a little boy had cried out, "It's Sophia the shepherd-girl! He kept us waiting three months for her?"

Joseph waited again for the crowd to become quiet. "This is not what you expected, I know. But she is indeed the wisest and most royal creature in the world. She will be my counselor, my friend, my love, the mother of the kings who shall come after me. With her at my side, I shall become the wisest, most just king on earth. Sophia shall be the symbol of my reign."

Just then, Julius's lion strode proudly into the room and began to circle Joseph and Sophia. Joseph backed away, leaving Sophia to face the lion alone. The lords and ladies held their breath.

The lion lunged toward Sophia and roared, but Sophia stood unmoved. Without a word, she put out a small hand to stroke the lion's forehead. The lion jerked away, circled, and then came near again. Sophia touched him lightly on the head, spoke softly in his ear, gently smoothed his mane.

Minutes later, the lion lay down on the floor, yawned, and closed his eyes. Sophia caressed his head until he was fast asleep. Then she walked over to Joseph and kissed him.

King Lothar was amazed. Queen Emma was very happy. All of the twelve gentlemen agreed that Joseph's was truly the most wonderful and royal creature. Even Alexander and Julius agreed that Joseph had won the contest.

7

Eight days later, Joseph and Sophia were married. Joseph wore a long purple robe and Sophia, a flowing white dress with jewels of every kind woven into the cloth. And, when King Lothar died, Joseph became king and ruled wisely and justly ever after, with the lovely Sophia at his side.

MORAL

The beginning of wisdom is:
Acquire wisdom; and with all your acquiring,
get understanding. Prize her, and she will exalt
you; she will honor you if you embrace her.
She will place on your head a garland of grace;
she will present you with a crown of beauty.
(Prov. 4:7-9)

Chapter II

simon and the fruit vendor

here was once a young man named Simon who wanted, as all young men do at one time or another, at least in fairy tales, to go into the world to make his fortune. Early one morning, Simon gathered his few belongings and went to say goodbye to his father.

"Father, I am leaving home to go into the world to make my fortune," he said. Simon used precisely these words because he, like you, had been reading fairy tales all his life.

His father looked out the window, smiling sadly as if remembering some event of the distant past. He drew a deep breath, then spoke. "Very well, son. But stay a moment while I tell you some things I have learned. You may find them useful. You are going to the city?"

"Yes, Father."

"Then, I must tell you that there are some very dishonest fellows in the city. If anyone tempts you to follow evil, do not go with him. Do you promise?"

"Yes, Father."

"Let your eyes look directly ahead of you. Watch where your feet are walking. Do not turn to the right or left. Then you will prosper. Do you understand?"

"Yes, Father." Simon looked out the window. How late it was getting, and he was still not on the road!

"And there are dishonest women as well. Be careful whom you choose as your companions. Do you swear?"

"I do, Father," the young man said, though he was only half listening. He waited for his father to say more. After a moment, he asked, "Is that all, Father?"

"That is all."

"Then I shall be going." Simon kissed his father, picked up his pack, and left.

The city lay a three-day walk to the north. On the first day, Simon passed an old man driving an ox cart.

"Going to the city?" asked the old man. When Simon nodded, the old man said, "Hop on the wagon. I'm going there myself. I'm selling pies at the fair." There was something strangely frightening about the old man's crackling voice.

Remembering his father's words, the young man kept his eyes fixed on the road in front of him. "No. No, thank you. I shall walk." Without stopping, he walked straight past the ox cart and on toward the city.

The second day, Simon passed a group of men gathered at the side of the road. One, who had a black bag over his shoulder, called to him as he walked by, asking if he were headed for the city.

Simon stopped in the road. "Yes, I am. Why do you ask?"

"We're going to the city too. To make some money." Another of the men snickered and the speaker slapped him with

12

the back of his hand. "We need at least one more to work with us," he added, glaring at his companions.

Simon cast a sideways glance. "What kind of work?"

This time the man with the bag over his shoulder snickered, and his fellows joined in. "Aren't you the curious one? I can't tell you much. Only that you'll make money—a lot of money."

Simon remembered his father's words, which for a few moments he had completely forgotten. Looking straight ahead, he answered, "No. No, thank you. I must go to the city myself." He walked straight past the gang of thieves—for that is what they were—and on toward the city.

The sun was beginning to go down when Simon arrived at the gate of the city on the third day of his journey. At the gate were two young women, selling goods from wagons and shouting to everyone who passed by. The young man stopped to see what they were selling.

The first young woman, tall and slender as a tree, wore a ragged dress, gray as dry earth. Small animals and birds huddled at her feet, as if seeking shade in her shadow. Her face was smeared with mud, and she had dirt under her fingernails, as if she had been digging in a garden. "Fruit! Fruit for sale!" she cried when she saw Simon.

"What kind of fruit do you have?" he asked politely.

"I have every fruit you can imagine. It is the most delicious fruit you will ever eat. Come, buy my fruit!"

Simon peered into the wagon. The apples and pears looked old and bruised. The grapes were shriveled like raisins, the plums like prunes.

As he looked at the fruit, Simon realized the second young woman had come up behind him.

13

"My," he heard her say. "What a handsome man you are!"

The boy blushed and looked at the ground. When he looked up, he saw before him the most beautiful face he had ever seen. Her skin was smoother than oil, her hair black as a raven. She was wearing a purple dress, as a princess might. At that very moment, the boy forgot his father's instructions.

"What are you selling?" he stammered.

"Gold, silver, jewels." Her words were as sweet and thick as brown honey. "Come, look. And buy."

The boy peered into her wagon. It was filled with trinkets and jewelry that sparkled so brightly in the late afternoon sun that he had to cover his eyes.

"Do these please you?" the woman asked. When he nodded, she said, "I have many more jewels at home. Would you like to come see them?"

Before Simon could answer, the fruit vendor interrupted, "Don't go with her! She's dangerous, and the men who follow her come to great harm!" The boy looked at her with a puzzled frown. "Besides," she continued, "my fruit is better than gold. Come, buy from me!"

But the woman dressed like a princess answered, "Don't listen to her. Look at me. Do I look dangerous? Believe what you see. And look at her! She's dirty and dressed in rags, and her fruit is old and dry. She's just mad because she cannot sell her rotten fruit, but I sell my jewels to everyone. She's jealous because I have more buyers than she."

Simon thought a moment, and then laughed at the fruit vendor. "Your fruit better than gold? I've seen better fruit rotting on the ground!" Turning to the jewel seller, he said, "I would like to see more jewels. Please take me to your

14

house." So taking hold of the wagon, he followed her through the city gate.

As he walked away, the boy heard the fruit seller call to him, "You will come to harm! Turn back!" He was not listening. She cried again, "Remember this day! I called to you and you refused. I stretched out my hand to help you but you paid no attention. Trouble will come upon you like a storm and whirlwind. You should have listened to me! Then I would have given you everything you desired. You should have listened!"

"Don't mind her," the jewel seller said when they had turned a corner. "She's a fool who thinks she's wise."

As they turned the corner, she stumbled and nearly fell. Simon caught her by the arm.

"Thank you," she said. "I'm afraid I'm unsteady on my feet sometimes. Could you please hold me up?"

Simon held her arm and pushed the wagon as they walked up and down the twisting streets of the city. As they walked, the boy kept glancing at the princess that walked beside him. To think that she was not only beautiful, but very rich. Perhaps, he thought, she will fall in love with me as I have already fallen in love with her.

The sky was dark by the time they turned into a narrow alley. At the end of alley they came to a set of broken steps that stretched down to a basement. At the bottom, a door was barely visible.

"Is this your home?" Simon asked nervously.

"Yes. Come down the steps, and I will show you around. You do want to see more jewels, don't you?"

The boy felt a sharp pain, as if an arrow had pierced his heart. He was not sure whether the pain was love or fear or both or something else altogether. Looking to the starlit sky

15

to gather his courage, he followed the princess down into the darkness. She unlocked the door and handed him a lamp.

"Go in," she commanded.

The boy ducked through the small door into a damp cellar. He held up the lamp, expecting to be dazzled by a room full of gold and silver and jewels. Instead, the walls were covered with something shiny and green. A rat scampered behind a pile of garbage. The sickening odor of death was so strong Simon could almost see it. Propped against the far wall was a human skeleton.

Simon turned, opening his mouth to cry out. Before he could turn around, he heard the heavy sound of the door closing, the scrape of a rusty lock, and the light dance of footsteps ascending the broken stairs outside. He ran to the door and tried the handle. It didn't move. He pounded and cried for help. No answer came. In a few moments, the lamp flickered and went out. The boy sank to the floor and began to cry.

As he touched the floor, Simon felt something hard next to his hand. He picked it up and held it under his nose. The smell of moldy bread burned his nostrils, and he threw the loaf across the room.

"Oh, I wish I had remembered my father's instructions! I wish I had listened to the fruit vendor instead of wanting to look at gold and silver! But I wouldn't listen! And look where it got me!" He cried until he could cry no longer. Then, being as exhausted as he was afraid, he fell asleep.

When Simon awoke, the door was framed by a dim line of sunlight. He was enormously hungry. Crawling on his hands and knees, he was able to find the loaf of bread he had tossed away the night before. Holding his breath, he broke off a piece, chewed, and swallowed it.

17

He imagined what he would be doing if he were at his father's house. Breakfast would be just beginning, and the table would be nearly breaking under the load of eggs, sausage, bowls of fruit, cups of milk, bread and rolls still warm and fragrant from the oven. "I have nothing but a moldy loaf of bread," he thought, and he began to cry again.

Through days and nights, Simon wept, slept, and ate moldy bread. Three or four nights later, he was awakened about midnight by the sound of scratching on the wall across the room. At first, he thought it was a rat. The sound grew louder and louder. He huddled in the corner, his mind a whirlwind of fear.

The scratching stopped, and in the dark he sensed that a figure had emerged from the wall. He stared across the room. "Who's there?" he whispered, his voice cracking.

The figure crept closer and closer. Just when he was about to scream, however, a gentle voice said, "Don't be afraid. I have come to help," and Simon recognized the fruit vendor whom he had met at the city gate days before. At the sound of her voice, his heart came alive with hope. He strained his ears, hoping she would speak again. For a few moments, he heard nothing, and he began to think he might have imagined it all. Then she came near and touched his hand.

"You are filthy," she said quietly. The next thing Simon knew, cold water was streaming over his hands and head. He closed his eyes as it flooded over his face, into his mouth, down his back.

When he opened his eyes, the room seemed lit by a warm white light. The young woman before him was no longer dressed in rags, but in a flowing dress that seemed to fill the whole room. The dress was white as light and sparkled with

18

jewels of every description. "Like a bride adorned for her husband" was the thought that crossed Simon's mind.

Before he could even thank her, she offered him a brownish, bruised pear. Realizing that even a brown pear was better than moldy bread, Simon took the fruit greedily. Its taste was sweeter than honey in the honeycomb. Its juice warmed his throat like wine and trickled down his chin.

Laughing in amazement, Simon said, "This is the best fruit I have ever tasted!"

The fruit vendor nodded with a grave smile. "Eat quickly. Put on your shoes. We must leave before she returns."

"Why did she bring me here?" he asked as he struggled with his boots, his mouth still full of fruit. (It is well known that even the most polite people may forget their manners after being imprisoned for days with nothing but moldy bread to eat.)

"Do you think she could afford those expensive clothes by selling jewelry at the city gate? Oh, no. She is not what she appears to be. She is not rich because she is a seller of jewels. She is a seller of men!"

"I was to be a slave." Simon whispered to himself.

"You still might be if you don't hurry," the fruit vendor said earnestly.

Simon followed her to the other side of the room where he found a tunnel through the wall. Slender as a tree, she easily climbed into the hole and crawled away into the darkness. But the tunnel seemed too small for Simon. He hesitated for a moment. He did not like tight spaces anyway. Still, knowing he had to escape, he entered the tunnel, where he squirmed and scratched and slowly followed her through the long passageway. After what seemed like hours of labor,

19

the tunnel turned upward, and a growing spot of light appeared in front of them.

When they climbed out of the tunnel, the morning sun was shining overhead. They were in a park in the middle of the city. Birds sang in the trees and fluttered around the fruit vendor, landing on her shoulders and pulling playfully at her hair. The green hillside shimmered with dew. For Simon, it was like being reborn into a new world.

"Come," said the fruit vendor. "If you are staying in the city, we must find you a change of clothes and a place to live." Taking Simon by the hand, she led him up the hill, and they disappeared over the sunlit peak.

And I've heard reports—from very reliable sources, mind you—that they were soon married and lived happily ever after.

MORAL

Wisdom shouts in the street,
she lifts her voice in the square; at the head of
the noisy streets she cries out; at the entrance
of the gates of the city, she utters her sayings:
"How long, O naive ones, will you love
simplicity? . . . Turn to my reproof; behold, I
will pour out my spirit on you; I will make my
words known to you."
(Prov. 1:20-23)

20

Chapter III

ᴄʜᴇ ʙʟᴇᴇᴅɪɴɢ ᴄʀᴇᴇ

nce upon a time, an oak tree stood on a hill over-looking a quiet valley. The tree was tall for his age and very strong. His long branches spread in every direction, and his leaves sparkled like emeralds in the sunlight. Where his branches met his thick trunk, robins and gray squirrels built their nests.

On the other side of the valley was a temple of unearthly beauty. It was so wondrous a temple that the tree often doubted that men could have built it. It must have fallen from the sky. Every morning and evening a song drifted from the temple, a song so pure it filled the heart with a painful joy.

The tree gazed each day at the temple of unearthly beauty and listened to the song that filled the heart with a painful joy. He was saddened when night fell, hiding the temple in darkness, and he was delighted when the morning sunlight unveiled the temple anew. He felt lonely in the evening when the song faded to silence, and he thrilled when it began again each day at daybreak and sunset. He dreamed of a world where there would be no night and where the song would never end. He wanted to gaze and listen forever.

But the more the tree looked at the temple and the more he listened to the song, the more he knew he would never be content with looking and listening, even if he could look and listen for all eternity. Deep in his heart, he did not want to gaze at the temple. He wanted to become the temple, to surround the hushed space of the inner sanctuary, where even children spoke in whispers. Deep in his heart, he did not want to listen to the song. He wanted to become the song, to spread himself over the valley like a blanket of music softer than silence.

Thinking these thoughts made the tree sadder still. For he was a tree, and he knew he would never be a temple of unearthly beauty or a song that filled the heart with a painful joy. His branches were too twisted, his bark too rough, the voice of the wind through his leaves too harsh and hollow.

So, for many years, the tree stood on his hill, gazing and listening. His heart grew sadder with each passing year. In what seemed like a very short time, he was no longer a young tree. And still he wished nothing more than to become the temple of unearthly beauty and to be the song that filled the heart with a painful joy.

One night, the temple hill was lighted as if it were day. An orange glow flickered against the black sky, growing brighter, then nearly disappearing. Through the cool night air, the tree heard a distant voice cry, "Fire!"

When the sun rose the next morning, the valley was utterly still. The mockingbirds refused to sing. No squirrels scampered chattering through the treetops. Worst of all, where the temple had been there was only a smoking black ruin. Men circled the ruins with their hands thrust deep in their pockets, their heads bowed. Women sat on the grass with their faces in their hands.

The tree was sickened to see what had happened to the temple. Knowing he could no longer gaze at the temple or listen to its song, he felt more empty and alone than ever.

For several days, the men circled the ruins and the women sat on the grass. Then one day, the men stopped circling to huddle together, and the women drew their faces from their hands and looked up. The men talked and nodded and pointed excitedly. Smiles crossed the women's faces.

Across the valley, the tree watched with growing wonderment. The next day, he watched the men and women work in the midst of the black ruins, knocking over the remaining walls and picking up charred pieces of the temple's furniture. In a few days, the ruin was gone. All that remained of the temple was a black stain on the green hillside.

Then the men slung belts filled with shining tools across their shoulders and started down the hill toward the forest where the tree stood watching. They disappeared into the valley, and then reappeared near the tree. Soon they were circling the trees with their hands in their pockets.

The tree was startled by a shout that came from somewhere near his trunk. "This one looks ready!" a man cried to his friends. In a moment the tree was surrounded, and the men were running their hands up and down his bark. It tickled, but the tree was afraid to laugh.

The men talked and nodded. Then all but one ran back into the forest. The remaining man took a stick with a bright metal head from his belt, stamped his feet, twisted his back away from the tree, and swung the stick.

The blow shook the tree from his topmost branches down to his roots. In shock and surprise, he cried out, but no one seemed to hear. He felt a stinging pain low on his trunk as the shining tool made another gaping wound, then another. Strips of bark peeled away like the skin of an apple. The tree felt sap flowing from his wound.

23

"Look at this," the man cried. "This sap looks red. Like blood! I've never seen anything like this before. It's a bleeding tree!" The other men came closer and circled the tree with their hands in their pockets, nodded, and then scampered back to their hiding places in the forest.

The man swung his shining tool again and again. After a while, he became tired, and another man took the stick and began swinging it on the other side of the trunk. The tree shuddered in agony with each blow. He felt himself weakening as his trunk was slowly cut off from his roots.

All the men took turns striking the tree with the shining tool. Finally, the tree could no longer stand and began to sway. The men cried out and ran deeper into the forest as the tree, losing all strength, fell to the ground with a thunderous crash.

No use trying to get up, the tree thought. Perhaps if I lie here, they will leave me alone and go away. Before he had finished that thought, the men had come out of the forest, each carrying a shining tool of his own. They pushed their way through the branches toward the trunk and swung their tools against the branches. One by one, branches were torn from trunk. At each branch, red sap dripped onto the ground.

The man who had first swung his shining tool against the tree cut off a thick branch. "This is good strong wood," he shouted to his friends. "We could probably use this branch in the organ." To the tree, it sounded as if the man was shouting from the far end of a long tunnel.

From the tree's higher branches, a voice answered, "These smaller branches are strong too. We can make pipes and flutes and violins from these."

In no time, the tree's branches had all been removed. The tree no longer felt pain, only a numbness like death. Perhaps

25

they wanted only the branches, he thought. Now they will leave me alone and let me die in peace.

No sooner had he finished that thought than he felt strong hands tying ropes to his trunk. It seemed to be happening to someone else, the tree thought. His mind drifted into a kind of sleep. He was jerked awake as the men bowed their backs to pull his branchless trunk down into the valley. They pulled again and again. Finally, the tree felt himself rolling, rolling down the hill, faster and faster. The men scattered in all directions, picked up their tools, and came running to catch up.

At the bottom of the hill, the tree came to a rest. Still dizzy from rolling, he heard the pounding of feet as the men bounded down the hill after him. Then they took hold of the ropes and pulled him toward a long house without walls that stood beside the river that flowed through the valley.

Grunting and groaning, the men pulled what was left of the tree into the long house, and lifted him over a deep pit. Looking up, the tree saw two men holding a long metal strip, covered with sharp teeth. He was too weak to move, and could only watch in terror as the men pulled the toothed metal back and forth across his trunk. It cut into his trunk as the teeth of a wolf tear a helpless sheep. Dust flew in all directions. The tree tried to cry out, to stand up, to roll off the table. But it was no use. Crying out with a loud voice, he fainted—or perhaps died.

The tree knew nothing of what happened next. After his trunk was sawn into boards, the boards were cut and trimmed. Corners were squared, and the boards were sanded smooth. Then they were polished to a golden shine. Small branches were cut, hollowed out, and carved into pipes and flutes. Larger branches were cut, bent, carved, and polished to make other instruments. The largest branches were cut into boards for an organ.

The tree never knew how long he had slept or fainted or died or whatever it was that had happened to him. When he first awoke, he did not know where he was. After the pain he had endured, he was amazed to find himself alive. Slanting rays of morning sunlight, changed into a rainbow by stained glass windows, filled the air. Everywhere he looked, his eyes were dazzled by the sights. In front of him, the tree saw a wooden pillar carved with great cunning, and the tree recognized it as one of his friends from the forest.

Far below him, men, women, and children sat in restless silence, waiting for something or someone. Then there was music, played softly at first, then louder and louder. The tree recognized the flutes, violins, and organ as his own branches. The people began to sing.

And then the tree knew. He had been made into the inner wall of a new temple of unearthly beauty and that his branches had become a song so pure it filled the heart with a painful joy.

MORAL

*My son, do not reject the discipline of the
LORD, or loathe His reproof, for whom the
LORD loves He reproves, even as a father, the
son in whom he delights.*
(Prov. 3: 11–12)

Chapter IV

BAREFOOT MESSENGER

ne day, a king summoned his chief servant to his throne. When the servant appeared, he had been burning leaves in the king's forest. His clothes smelled so strongly of smoke that the king's eyes began to water.

Wiping his eyes with a silk handkerchief, the king handed the servant a scroll. "Deliver this to the king on the other side of the high mountains," he commanded. "It is a request from my son the prince to marry the king's daughter. If the king and his daughter agree, you shall stay to prepare her for the wedding. Teach her our tongue and customs, guard her until the wedding, and then bring her back to present her as the next queen of this realm. If they do not agree, you will return immediately to give me their answer. To get to the king's castle, you must walk straight toward the rising sun."

"Sire, I have heard of that kingdom," the servant replied as he took the scroll. "It is a very long journey."

"Yes. It is a very long journey," answered the king.

"And the way across the high mountains is too steep for any horse to travel."

"Yes, you must walk."

"Then, Sire, I will need an extra pair of shoes," the servant said.

"No, you do not need another pair of shoes. You need no shoes at all. Walk barefoot on the narrow footpath that leads around the great forest."

"Your Highness, I have heard about that footpath. It is narrow and hard, full of sharp rocks."

"Do as I say. Take no shoes with you. You will not be harmed."

The king gave the servant two bags. "In the first is money to help you along the way," he said. "In the other are rings and necklaces to adorn the princess. Protect these with your life. Tell no one why you are travelling. Swear to me that you will do as I say."

"I swear it," the servant said.

"Then go," the king said as he filled the servant's hands with the two bags.

The servant bowed, took the bags, and left the king. Walking barefoot around the great forest and over the high mountains was not very appealing to him. But he was a servant, so he reminded himself that his duty was to obey the king. Leaving his shoes behind, he started off toward the rising sun.

He walked all day along the footpath. By evening, his feet were sore and bleeding. The big toe of his right foot was swollen where he had stubbed it on a rock, and the little toe of his left foot was bruised from an encounter with a tree root. When it was too dark to go on, he limped to an inn, asked for a room, and sat down to eat.

While the servant was eating dinner, a small man with a pointed hat and a patchy beard sat down next to him.

"You are travelling, are you not?" the man whispered to the servant, leaning close. His breath smelled so strongly of onions that it made the servant's eyes water.

"I am. I have an important message to deliver to the king on the other side of the high mountains," the chief servant said, forgetting the king's command.

"I see. A message from whom?" When the little man smiled, the servant saw he had only three teeth, two of them dark brown and the other a shade of green the servant had never seen before.

"I cannot say." The servant was suddenly afraid of the little man. He stood up and began to move to another table.

"I see you are limping," said the small man. "And no wonder. You have no shoes."

"I need no shoes," the servant answered, though his answer sounded more like a question.

"No? I think you do. And you are in luck. I am a maker and seller of shoes."

The servant sat down again. "Are you?" he asked, a little too eagerly.

"My shoes are the best shoes in the world. They are comfortable. They never wear out. I even have some shoes with magical powers. But, since you need no shoes . . ."

"Magical powers? What kind of magical powers?"

The little man with the onion breath leaned close. "I have a pair of shoes that will guide you through the darkest parts of the great forest in the dead of night," he whispered. "Even if you are not able to see where you are going! You tell the shoes where you wish to go, and they will take you there."

"How wonderful!" The servant was almost giggling. What great good luck to have stopped at the very same inn where this shoemaker was staying!

31

The man found a pair of shoes that fit the servant perfectly, and the servant pulled his moneybag from his belt to pay for them. "My, that is a fine looking purse," the little man said.

"Oh, it is nothing really. I have a couple of them." The little man smiled his ugly grin and nodded knowingly.

The next day the servant started out on his journey wearing his new magical shoes. They seemed to heal all his cuts and bruises. His feet stopped hurting. All day long he walked without stubbing his toe. By night, when he stopped at another inn, he was no longer limping.

While the servant was eating dinner at the inn the second night, a tall man with a flat hat and a thick beard sat down at the table.

"You are travelling, are you not?" the tall man whispered, putting a heavy hand on the servant's shoulder. His hands smelt so strongly of vinegar that the servant's eyes watered.

"I am. I have an important message to deliver to the king on the other side of the high mountains."

"That is a very long journey." When the tall man smiled, the servant noticed that his teeth were white as goose down.

"Yes," the servant said. He was suddenly very tired. "It is a very long journey."

"I know a shorter way to get there. There is a highway through the great forest. A very wide highway, very easy to travel."

"I am not going through the great forest," the servant said angrily. Afraid of the tall man, he stood and began to move to another table.

"It might take weeks to go around the great forest. But it only takes one day to go through. But, since you must stay on the footpath . . ."

32

The servant sat down and began to count the days. "I suppose if it would save me some time, that could only be for the good."

The next morning, the tall man showed the servant the entrance to the highway through the great forest. The sun was high overhead when he entered the wood, but the thick trees kept the air cool and fresh. The highway was smooth and wide. He walked quickly, watching the squirrels as they leaped from tree to tree overhead. This was a better path than the narrow, rocky path around the forest, he decided.

After he had walked for many hours, it began to grow dark, but the servant still could not see the end of the highway through the great forest. Darker and darker it became until it was night. No light from moon or stars shone through the leafy roof of the wood. The servant could not see his hand in front of his face, or the ground where he was walking. Fear slithered down his back like a cold snake.

Then he remembered what the shoemaker had told him about the magic shoes he was wearing. He sat down, took off his shoes, and told them to take him to the end of the forest highway. He put the shoes back on his feet and walked on, happy that he could not get lost.

For a time, the great forest was deathly still. An owl hooted as it glided through the air. A cricket chirruped from a bush. A gentle wind blew through the treetops. Then the forest became deathly still again.

As the servant walked past a huge oak tree, he heard new sounds—the sound of snapping twigs, then the crunch of a heavy boot on dead leaves. Someone was following him.

The servant quickly knelt down to remind his magic shoes where to go and to ask them to hurry up. Before he could stand, someone had jumped on his back and pushed him to the ground. A pair of hands grabbed his arms, and another his legs. Robbers! The robber on his back had breath that smelled of onions. The hands that held his arms smelled of vinegar.

The servant struggled, but it was no use. Six or eight strong hands were clamped tight to his arms and legs. Another pair of hands fumbled through his cloak for the bags the king had given him. He heard a heavy crack on the back of his head, and then he fell over in a heap.

When he awoke, flickering light was piercing through the tree branches swaying lazily in the morning breeze. He was in the middle of the great forest, and the highway was nowhere to be seen. When he heard a bush rustle behind him, he spun around, ready for another attack.

Behind him, sitting in front of a small fire, was the prince, his master's son. He was roasting a rabbit for breakfast. Beside him lay the two bags that the servant had been carrying. The prince was barefoot.

The servant ran to the prince, fell on his face, and held him by the knees. He sobbed, "I'm so sorry!" over and over. When he calmed himself, he asked the prince, "How did you get here?"

"My father sent me to follow you. He thought you might not do exactly as he had commanded, and he wanted to make sure that you were not harmed. He also wanted to make sure the rings and necklaces were taken safely to the daughter of the king over the high mountains."

"What happened to the robbers?"

"I watched you go into the great forest yesterday, as my father told me you would. I followed behind all day. When it became dark, I lighted a torch and stayed far behind. It was hard to keep up, with you wandering this way and that. You acted so strangely. You seemed to be stopping every so often to talk to the ground. Why did you think you could walk through the great forest at night?"

The servant said nothing, too embarrassed to tell the prince he had trusted the magic shoes.

"No matter," the prince said. "When the robbers attacked, I drove them away."

"Then all of the money and jewels are still here?"

The prince nodded.

The servant began to weep again. "I am sorry that I disobeyed your father. I am not worthy to be your servant. But I beg your grace, let me have another chance to prove I am a faithful servant. I will follow your instructions completely."

The prince smiled. He tore a leg from the rabbit and handed it to the servant. "Take, eat. It is a long way back to the footpath, and you have an even longer journey ahead of you."

They walked through the great forest all day. When it grew dark, the prince lighted his torch and led the way out of the shadowy forest. Just as the sun was peeking over the horizon, the prince led the servant back to the narrow footpath.

"I am returning to my father," the prince said. "I trust you shall not come to harm again on this journey."

"No, I think not," said the servant.

"Bring my bride to me safely, then. I shall feast with you again on my wedding day." The prince turned and walked toward his father's house. The next moment he was out of sight.

The servant knelt and took off his magical shoes and threw them to the side of footpath. Then he limped on barefoot along the narrow road toward the rising sun.

MORAL

*The way of the righteous is like
the first gleam of dawn, shining ever brighter
until the full light of day; but the way of the
wicked is like deep darkness; they do not
know what makes them stumble.
(Prov. 4:18-19)*

Chapter V

ROBIN AND
THE MASTER'S WIFE

nce upon a time, there was a young man named Robin who served a great prince. The prince lived in a mansion with many rooms and passageways and owned much land.

Robin had charge of all his master's gardens and lands. Day after day, he rode from one end of the estate to the other, making sure that everyone and everything was working. When a mule died, the master sent Robin to market with a bag of silver to buy another, and Robin returned with most of the silver, as well as a fine new mule. At the beginning of each month, the prince sent Robin to collect rent from the peasants who worked in the fields. If some of the rent was missing, Robin would have to pay the difference himself, but none was ever missing.

On the master's estate, no servant was given more responsibility nor was any servant more faithful than Robin. No one, that is, save the prince's very old Chief Steward.

Soon after his ninetieth birthday, the Chief Steward died, and the prince had to choose someone to take his place. He called Robin to his chamber, along with another servant, whose name was Joseph.

"My Chief Steward, who served me faithfully for many years, is dead," the master began. "Now I must choose another Chief Steward in his place. I want a Chief Steward who will free me from every care for my house and my estates, so I can spend my time in reading and study and hunting. I have decided to choose one of you two as my new Steward. Do you wish to help me decide whom to choose?"

"I am quite certain that Joseph would make a fine Chief Steward," Robin answered quickly. "He has been a faithful servant for—how long has it been? Nearly four years?"

"It has been only two, as you well know," Joseph answered. "But Robin has been a servant much longer. It is true he knows very little about the house, its needs, or its servants, but he would be a splendid Chief Steward nonetheless."

"I am honored you hold me in such high esteem," Robin said modestly. "And, though Joseph has never worked in the fields, and though he might have a difficult time buying a mule from the traders in town, he would, I am certain, be the best Chief Steward in the land."

Robin and Joseph went on and on for some time, giving each other compliments that did not quite sound like compliments.

"Enough!" cried the prince. "I have made my decision. Robin will be the new Chief Steward."

Robin could scarcely believe his ears. Through all his years of service, he had had a secret ambition to be Chief Steward of the prince's estates. Now his dream had come true.

"But Joseph is right." The master's voice interrupted Robin's pleasant thoughts. "You have never lived in the house and have much to learn. Come, I will show you around and explain your duties."

At the kitchen, the prince stopped and said, "Whatever you wish to eat from the kitchen, it is yours. Whatever food or drink you wish to buy in preparation for my feasts, you may buy." He showed Robin the garden in the central courtyard and said, "I give you all the flowers and plants, to decorate the house and lawns as you desire." He presented Robin before the guards and servants and said, "You are in charge of them all." After showing Robin everything in his house, the prince said, "You will rule it all. I give it all into your hands as my Chief Steward."

"But . . ." The prince's jolly face became very serious. "You may never go into the west wing. That is forbidden to all servants. And it is your job to make sure no one else goes into the west wing either. You must guard it even with your life."

Robin took up his duties as Chief Steward with great energy. Fields and farmlands he knew well, and he quickly mastered the difficult jobs of managing the most stubborn household servants, of buying enough food and drink to satisfy everyone but not so much that it spoiled, and of keeping track of how the prince's every penny was being spent.

The first feast he prepared as Chief Steward was declared by Lord Andrew of Bostwich the most imaginative feast ever given in the eastern provinces. Because he made wise purchases, Robin was able to save a good deal of the master's money. With what he saved, Robin had the broken stones of one of the towers repaired. He hired skilled workmen to carve cunning designs in the tall front door and wise craftsmen to cast two majestic bronze pillars to set on either side of the entrance.

One day, as Robin was hurrying down one of the halls, he saw the master's beautiful wife peering at him around the corner of the west wing. Through all his years as a servant, Robin had seen the prince's wife only a few times, and only from a great distance. On this occasion, he was close enough to sense the sweet warmth of her perfume and to look into her eyes, which sparkled like the silver fish hook that dangled from the end of her long necklace.

Robin stopped and stared. Her beauty was so startling that Robin had to gasp for breath. The master's wife smiled and lowered her eyelids. Then laughing loudly, she turned and, silk skirts rustling behind her, entered a room and closed the door.

After that day, Robin's heart was full of the beauty of the master's wife, and he found many reasons to walk past the west wing. One day, after looking all around to make sure he was not watched, Robin tiptoed up the main hallway of the west wing, listening intently at each door. Behind the third door, he heard the voices of two ladies, one of which he recognized as belonging to the master's wife. He could not understand her words, but he was enchanted by her smooth and soothing voice and captivated by her robust laughter.

Some days later, Robin chanced to be walking through the central garden in the courtyard of the prince's home. As he stepped into the garden, he noticed the master's wife sitting on a stone bench, wearing a red dress. A fragile, net-like scarf hung from her neck over her heart. When Robin went to her, she looked up and smiled.

"I have been watching you," she said sweetly. "I sit at my window watching you through the lattice whenever you ride away."

42

"I have been watching for you too." Robin could hardly believe it was he who spoke.

"I have even followed you through the streets of town, when you go to buy wine."

"And I have dreamed of you." Robin felt he was dreaming even now. "The master is away today, isn't he?" Robin heard his voice ask the question but immediately wished he had said nothing.

She laughed at his embarrassment. "Yes. Bird hunting or something. Everyone went with him. There is no one in the house. No one at all." She straightened the skirt of her dress. "I love red. It is a delight to the eyes, don't you think?" She laughed again.

Before Robin had a chance to agree, the master's wife caught him by the hand. Her slender fingers held his wrist like chains. She whispered in his ear, "I came to the garden hoping to meet you, and now we are together. Let's go to my chambers. You have never been to my chambers, have you? I have made special preparations today. My couch is spread with silk and linen coverings, and the room smells of myrrh and cinnamon. Come with me."

Robin tried to pull away. "I have served my master for many years, and I have never disobeyed him. He has been generous and good to me. He has given all he has into my charge. I do not want to. . . . He told me not. . . ."

"But you do want to, don't you?" she asked. Robin made a half-hearted effort to flee. Tightening her grip on his wrist, she asked, "Did not my master give all he has into your hands? Is it fair that he withheld me from you? He will not be home for many days. He will never know."

Robin looked into her sparkling eyes. Smiling dumbly like an ox, Robin followed her to her chambers in the west wing.

44

The master's wife closed the door quietly behind them, turned, threw her arms around Robin's neck, and kissed him. Robin kissed her too.

While they were still in their embrace, there was a pounding at the door and the thundering voice of the master, "Robin, are you in there?"

Robin looked everywhere for a place to hide and finally jumped under the silk covering on the couch. It was a stupid place to hide, but before he could escape, the master's wife, laughing loudly, opened the door, and her husband, dressed in black, stormed in like a thundercloud.

"What are you doing here?" he demanded of Robin.

Robin rolled off the couch and stood up, holding the silk in front of him, as if it would protect him from the prince's wrath. "Your wife, sir. She tempted me and led me in here," he said in a trembling voice.

"I told you not to come into the west wing! You are supposed to guard this wing! You are supposed to guard her! I gave you everything you could want! I withheld only my wife from you! And now this!"

The prince's round merry face was aflame with anger, and his voice was like a clap of thunder. "If you had stolen from me, I would understand! But this! You have no sense! No sense at all!"

Robin knelt before the prince, hoping for mercy, but the prince was in not in a mood to forgive.

"Curse you!" the prince thundered at his wife. Then to Robin he bellowed, "Curse you too! You will pay for this! You will pay dearly!"

The prince called for his guards, who seized Robin and led him to the garden in the central courtyard. Sweat moistened Robin's forehead as he sat watching the guards kindle a roaring fire. When the fire had burned down to flickering coals, the master appeared.

"Take off your shirt!" he commanded. As Robin stood and began to pull off his shirt, he noticed the prince was holding a whip made of twisted branches from a thorn tree. "Bend over and hold the bench," the prince ordered. Thirty-nine stinging blows fell on Robin's back.

"Now. Remove your boots!" the prince ordered. Trembling like a leaf in the wind, Robin did as his master commanded.

"Do you think you can walk on hot coals and not be burned?" the master asked. Robin stared but said nothing. "We shall see, then. Walk across the coals!"

At first, Robin did not believe the prince was serious, but a glance at his master's eyes told him this was no joking matter. Feeling as if he were dreaming, Robin put a toe into the bed of hot coals and quickly pulled it back.

"Walk! Walk!" the master shouted. Two guards came beside Robin, grasped his wrists like chains, and pulled him toward the fire. Stumbling, his feet pressed onto the glowing coals. When he got to the other side, he sank to his knees. His feet were black and blistered, his mind scorched with pain.

The master threw his boots at him. "Now, go! Never return to this house. You are cast out forever!"

Limping, Robin left the garden, stumbled through the carved door and past the tall bronze pillars. He glanced behind him and saw two guards stationed at the door to prevent his return. And as he walked down the lane away from the house, he thought the wind carried to his ear the sound of a woman's laughter.

MORAL

Keep from the evil woman,
from the smooth tongue of the adulteress.
Do not desire her beauty in your heart,
nor let her catch you with her eyelids.
For on account of a harlot one is reduced
to a loaf of bread, and an adulteress hunts
for the precious life.
(Prov. 7:24-26)

Chapter VI

The FARMER'S TREASURE

A farmer was once plowing his field when the plow hit something buried in the earth. Pulling his horse to a stop, the farmer knelt to examine it. He dug until he uncovered a round, hard object. When he had pulled it from the ground, he rubbed the top with his shirt until he could see he was holding a golden globe that shone like the sun.

Leaving his horse and plow in the field, the farmer rushed back to his small cottage to show his wife, who stood at the stove stirring soup. "Look! Look!" the farmer shrieked as he crashed through the door. "I found it in the field!"

Startled by her husband's cries, his wife dropped her spoon into the soup. Her apron caught the handle of the kettle and when she turned around, soup spilled over the kitchen floor.

"Look at what you made me do!" she said angrily. "Why did you come in here screaming like a madman?"

Too excited to speak, the farmer held up the globe. Even in the dim light of the kitchen, it seemed to glow. The farmer's wife stopped in the middle of a sentence and stared in wonder.

Holding it as gently as a wounded bird, the farmer set the globe on the kitchen table, while his wife found a rag to clean it. After a few moments of scrubbing, she stepped back. Neither had ever seen anything like it before. They thought it must be something from a king's palace, though they had never even been close to a king's palace.

The globe sat on a small platform. The gold on the top half was as bright as a slice of the sun. Set in the gold were jewels that sparkled like stars and carved birds so white they looked like chips of the moon. The bottom half was dark green, covered with colorful paintings of strange animals and trees and flowers. The platform was deep blue, decorated with fish and porpoises.

"It's a world," the farmer gasped.

"Yes. And it's all ours," his wife answered.

For hours they sat examining every detail of the globe. When it was almost midnight, they agreed they would sell it to the jeweler. They would then have enough money to build a big new house in town, and they would never again rise before the sun to milk the cow, never again sweat in the fields through long and hot afternoons, never again lose a night's sleep looking after a mare giving birth. Their miserable little lives with all their miserable little duties would be gone forever. They would live like a king and queen.

Neither the farmer nor his wife got any sleep that night. Before the sun had risen the next morning, they were out of bed and dressed. The farmer harnessed his horse to the rickety carriage and set the globe, carefully wrapped in a sheet, on the seat.

50

When they got to town, the farmer tucked the globe under his arm and went to see the jeweler. His wife walked up and down the streets looking in shop windows.

The jeweler's shop was not open. After the farmer banged on the door ten or twenty times, a pointed face peeked through the curtained window.

"Read the sign," came a squeaky voice. "Not open until nine. Come back then." The pointed face disappeared.

The farmer banged again. "Please! I have something very valuable. I want you to look at it!"

"Come back at nine!" answered the squeaky voice.

"Of course, I could go to the jeweler's shop on the other side of town," the farmer said in a loud voice as he turned to go.

Behind him the farmer heard the lock turn and the bell on the door jingle. The jeweler stepped out wearing a striped nightshirt. "Come in, come in," he said. "Won't hurt to get an early start today."

Inside the shop, the farmer put the globe on the table and slowly unwrapped it. The jeweler picked it up carefully. He pinched a pair of glasses on his thin nose, and looked closely.

"Hmm." When the jeweler said "Hmm," it sounded like a mouse snoring. "Very heavy. Can see why you were in such a hurry to see me. Hmm." He held his ear close to the globe and shook it.

"Well?" The farmer was impatient. "Is it gold? Is it worth something? How much will you pay for it?"

"Have to look at it very carefully. Don't want to give you the wrong answer." The jeweler smiled a sour-looking smile. "Come back next month. Will tell you what I think."

The farmer's heart sank. "Next month!? Can't you tell me sooner?" The jeweler shook his head, still smiling his

52

sour smile. "Then I will have to come back next month," the farmer said sadly.

When the farmer got back to the carriage, he found his wife surrounded by packages wrapped in red, green, and yellow paper.

"What is all this?" the farmer demanded.

"Oh, just a few dresses, a few hats, a few new pairs of shoes, a few new . . ."

"A *few* new pairs of shoes!" the farmer exclaimed. "You have never had more than one pair of shoes before."

"That is true, husband. But now we are going to be rich. Remember, the world is ours." She giggled like a child. "I told the merchants we would be able to pay them soon. Very soon." She giggled again.

"Well, perhaps you are right," the farmer sighed. "But no more shopping, at least for a month." The farmer told his wife what the jeweler had said.

"Oh, you silly," his wife said. "That just means we have to wait another month to be rich."

The month passed slowly. Neither the farmer nor his wife could think of anything but the globe of gold. The farmer spent mornings sitting on the front porch of the cottage dreaming about how everyone would watch in envy as he strutted through town in a fine suit on his way to lunch with the mayor. In the afternoon, he sat at a table drawing pictures of his new house, being careful to include the servants' quarters and rose gardens. He sketched a picture of his new carriage with its leather seats. With a thick pencil, he scratched numbers on every corner of his paper, figuring how much he could afford to spend on the best food and drink, once he was rich.

His wife dreamed of watching a maidservant set the table with silver spoons and real china dishes. She had never seen real china, at least not up close, so she had to imagine what it would look like. She thought of gossiping with the other elegant ladies of the town, and she saw herself telling witty jokes that made the other ladies twitter in their teacups.

Meanwhile, the animals in the barn were left unfed. The plow was still sitting in the field where the farmer had left it on the day he found his treasure. The vegetable garden was overgrown with weeds. It was not that the farmer did not notice. It just did not matter any longer—now that he was going to be rich.

When the month was over, the farmer and his wife went back into town. The jeweler was sitting behind his counter when they came into the shop.

"Ah. You're back," the jeweler said in a voice filled with what sounded like pity.

"What have you found out?" the farmer asked.

"Some bad news. Some good news. Globe is not made of gold. Made of lead. The gold, only the cheapest paint. The jewels, bits of colored glass. The white birds carved from the most common stone. Globe is worth almost nothing."

The farmer staggered as if he had been hit on the head with a shovel. He did not have to imagine what this was like, since it had happened to him more than once. "You said there was good news?" His voice sounded strange in his own ears.

"Yes, yes. Good news." The jeweler stopped for a moment so that his next words would sound very important. It takes a great effort, you see, to sound important when your voice squeaks like a mouse. "Seen globes like this before.

54

Very clever. Outside, worth little. But hollow inside. Maybe something valuable inside."

"Then open it!" the farmer shouted.

"Hmm. Easier said than done. No keyhole. Secret opening. Cannot help you. Take it to locksmith."

Without even a thank you to the jeweler, the farmer grabbed the globe and dashed out the door, leaving his wife standing open-mouthed at the jeweler's counter. He raced across the street and was inside the locksmith's shop before the bell on the jeweler's door stopped jingling.

"Can you . . . open this?" he asked breathlessly.

The locksmith wiped his broad face with a fat hand. "Pray tell, how do you know it opens?"

"I don't. Not really. The jeweler . . . told me . . . it might."

"Ah." When he said "Ah," he sounded like an elephant yawning. "I have heard of these kinds of things. Yes, they were first used by the emperors of China to hide secret papers, official documents and so forth. Or was it Japan? India perhaps. In any case, I have read many times about such things. Yes, the concept, the idea is very familiar to me. I do believe it was Japan after all."

"Please open it," the farmer said impatiently.

"Oh, I am quite afraid that will take me some time. I have never, you understand, actually seen such an object—until just now, of course. If in fact this is such an object. But it will take me some time and effort. I will have to examine . . ."

"How long?"

"Ah. Come back in a month, and I will see what I can do. It does look Japanese, if you ask me."

Disappointed, the farmer returned to the carriage. He told his wife what the locksmith had said. "Then we will have to

55

wait another month to become rich," she said. "I am certain that there is something very valuable inside that globe."

The next month passed more slowly than the first. The farmer still could not keep his mind off the globe. He spent his mornings wondering how it might open, his afternoons wondering what might be inside, and his nights wondering what life would be like when he became rich.

Unplowed fields went unplanted. Chickens starved to death. The garden vegetables were choked out by weeds. His wife began to bake bread from wheat they had been saving for the winter.

When the month was over, the farmer and his wife returned to town to see what the locksmith had discovered. A bright smile crossed his face when they entered his shop. "Wonderful news!" he said in a booming voice. "I consulted my books and found many examples of this kind of treasure box. As it turns out, they were used in China, Japan, and India—all three. Though they seem to have first been used in . . ."

"What is the wonderful news?"

"Why, I have opened the globe!" The locksmith's face gleamed with a proud smile.

"And?" The farmer and his wife said together.

"And? Oh, yes. And this was inside." With a flourish, the locksmith held up two shiny red apples. They looked fresh and inviting, as if they had just been picked from a tree.

"Is that all?" the farmer's wife asked. "Are *they* made of gold?"

The locksmith laughed loudly. "No, ma'am. They are made of *apple*." The farmer and his wife sadly turned to go. "By the way, don't eat those two apples," they heard the locksmith say as the door closed behind them. "They look fine, but they may be poisonous. In Japan, the objects inside

56

these treasure boxes were sometimes deadly. That is what the latest research shows."

As the farmer rattled over the road back to the cottage, the farmer's wife began to laugh.

"What are you laughing about?" the farmer asked angrily. "I know I'm a fool. But please do not laugh at me."

"Oh, my dearest husband," his wife answered, hardly able to control herself. "I am not laughing at you. I'm laughing because I know why those apples were in the globe."

"And why is that?" the farmer asked.

"Why, they must be magic apples," his wife answered. "Don't give me that look. You didn't really believe that locksmith, did you? What does he know about apples or treasure boxes or anything? Why else would anyone put apples into that globe, unless they're magic? And how could apples stay so fresh in that thing for so long? Maybe they will make us live forever. Or maybe they will make us rich. Or maybe they will grant us three wishes. Or maybe when we eat them everything we touch will turn to gold, like old King What's-His-Name. Who knows? Maybe we can still have the world after all."

The farmer did not believe it at first, but the more he listened the more sense she made, and she finally convinced him. When they got home, they sat down at the kitchen table with the apples between them.

The farmer's wife took the largest apple, cut off a slice with a knife, and ate it. "It's delicious," she said. "Try some." Then she gave some of the fruit also to her husband with her; and he did eat.

Three days later, four men came to door of the farmer's cottage. The tailor, the cobbler, and the hatmaker were coming to collect money for the dresses, shoes, and hats the farmer's wife had bought. The other man owned the land where the farmer lived, and was coming to collect the rent, which had been unpaid for months.

The farmyard was lifeless. In the barn, the horses and cows were thin as skeletons. When the men knocked at the door, there was no answer. And when they pushed it open, they saw the farmer and his wife slumped over the kitchen table, dead.

Between them on the table were two half-eaten apples.

MORAL

He who works his land will have abundant
food, but he who pursues fantasies
lacks judgment.
(Prov.12:11)

Chapter VII

CHE MAGICAL WALNUT

nce upon a time, a poor woodsman lived in the middle of a forest on the same piece of land where his father and grandfather had lived. The woodsman worked very hard, but he remained poor because other people cheated him. He would spend half a day cutting down a tree, and the other half dragging it through the forest to the sawmill. But the greedy owner of the sawmill gave him only a few coins for his labors.

But the woodsman never complained or asked for more. Instead, he was happy and content. He had a roof over his head, which he had made himself. Even though he was poor, there always turned out to be just enough of everything to go around. Every morning at sunrise, he kissed his wife and children before he went off into the forest singing in a glad voice. At dark, he would come home whistling.

One day as the woodsman was getting ready to cut down a tree, a voice called to him from the treetop. He looked up to see a squirrel hunched on a high branch.

"Did you say something?" the woodsman asked.

59

"I said, please do not cut down my tree," the squirrel answered. "I have lived here all my life. My grandfather lived in this tree when it was little more than a sapling. My children will live here when I die. Please do not take away our home."

"I am sorry," the woodsman answered, "but I have a family too. I must feed and clothe them. I am a woodsman, and I make my living by cutting down trees and selling them to the sawmill. If I do not cut down trees, I will not be able to take care of my family."

"Sir, there are many other trees in the forest," the squirrel answered.

"Yes, but this is one of the best, as you well know."

The squirrel shook his tail for a moment. "Sir, I will make a deal with you."

"What kind of deal can you make?" the woodsman laughed.

"If you promise not to cut down my tree, I will tell you an amazing secret. I promise you, this secret is worth more than any tree, much, much more."

The woodsman ran his hand over the bark of the tree. It was a solid tree. It might bring him good money at the sawmill. But it was not every day that a squirrel was willing to tell secrets. Perhaps the squirrel did have something very, very important to tell him. Besides, the woodsman liked the squirrel and felt sorry for him. "Squirrels are often rude," he thought. "Very few call anyone 'Sir' or say 'Please' nowadays. This is the most polite squirrel I have ever met."

With that, the woodsman made his decision. "Fine. I will not cut down your tree. May your children's children live in it. Now tell me your secret."

60

"Do you see that young walnut tree there?" the squirrel asked, pointing his tail. "Go shake the trunk. You must shake it gently. See what happens."

The woodsman shook the young walnut tree as gently as he could. He was expecting a shower of gold or diamonds. But only a single nut fell at his feet.

He looked at the squirrel. "Is that all? A walnut? I can get plenty of walnuts from other trees."

"Trust me," the squirrel said. "The walnuts from this tree are special."

The woodsman was greatly disappointed. He had traded a tall, strong tree for a walnut. He was beginning to think that the squirrel was only pretending to be polite. Perhaps all the rumors about squirrels being dishonest creatures were true after all. But a promise was a promise. He would not cut down the squirrel's tree. Without picking up the nut, he turned to go.

"Sir, do not forget your walnut," the squirrel called after him.

The woodsman picked up the nut, thrust it into his pocket, and walked off to find another tree to cut down.

"There are plenty more," the squirrel called. "But take only one at a time. Only one." Then he disappeared into the top branches of the tree.

By the time the woodsman arrived home that night, he had forgotten about the walnut. After dinner, he read a book to his children, prayed with them, and tucked them into bed.

As he undressed, he felt a lump in his pocket and remembered the squirrel and the walnut. He took out the nut and examined it under a lamp. It was an ordinary looking walnut, slightly green. Without another thought, he put it on the sill of his window, turned out the lamp, and rolled into bed.

61

When all was quiet, and the woodsman and his family were fast asleep, the walnut began to shake. Then it rolled in a circle, faster and faster. Finally, when it was spinning like a top, the shell popped open, and a small fairy leaped out and looked around. With a flutter of her wings (for she was a girl fairy), the fairy darted into the kitchen and began to work as quietly as a kitten.

All that night, the fairy worked in the house and garden. She cleaned where the woodsman's wife had not had time to clean. When she touched the bowl of fruit on the table, the fruit doubled in size. When she flew through the garden, the beans and cabbages became larger and greener. As morning approached, she climbed back into the walnut, and walnut and fairy both vanished.

When the woodsman and his wife awakened in the morning, they found the house clean, the fruit basket full, and the garden flourishing. They were overjoyed at their good fortune, and more than a little puzzled that the garden had grown so much overnight. They could not explain what had happened, but they gave special thanks over their breakfast. The woodsman never noticed the walnut was gone from the sill.

Every morning for a week, the woodsman and his wife awoke to find the house clean. The vegetables in the garden continued to grow and grow. The woodsman's wife picked some of the best cabbages and sold them in the village square.

The woodsman did not think about the walnut again until he passed the squirrel's tree some time later. Seeing him walk by, the squirrel called, "Sir, are things well?"

"Yes, yes. Very well," the woodsman said, thinking again how polite the squirrel was.

"Didn't I tell you?"

"You mean, it was the walnut that brought us such blessing?"

The squirrel seemed to smile, and then shook his tail and scampered away. Before he disappeared into the higher branches, he called back, "You need to get another one every week. Just one."

The woodsman was not sure the squirrel was telling the truth. But what could it hurt? He went to the walnut tree and shook it gently. Another walnut dropped at his feet. When he got home that night, he put it on the window sill.

The next morning, everything was clean and shiny. The vegetables in the garden were even larger and better than they had been the last time. When the woodsman looked at the window sill, he noticed the walnut was gone.

And so it went week after week. Every week, the woodsman went to the walnut tree, shook it gently, and took a single walnut to place on his window sill. His wife sold the vegetables in town, and the woodsman was able to save some coins, which he carefully hid behind a loose brick on the hearth.

One day, the sawmill owner's son was walking through the forest when he heard voices on the other side of a bush. Creeping closer, he saw the woodsman talking with the squirrel.

"The walnuts are bringing me blessings of every kind," the woodsman was saying. "Every one of the fairies has worked very hard. How can I ever thank you?"

"Sir, you have already paid me back, by being kind enough not to cut down my tree," the squirrel answered.

The sawmill owner's son had noticed the woodsman and his family looked fatter than ever before. He had eaten some of the cabbages and potatoes from the woodsman's garden, and he thought they were the very best he had ever tasted. Now he knew the secret of the woodsman's sudden prosperity. He watched as the woodsman shook the tree and picked up a walnut, and then he hurried back to tell his father.

After hearing about the magical walnut tree, the greedy sawmill owner smiled slyly and scratched his chin. He was thinking how rich he would be if he could get fairies to work for him. "I shall talk to the woodsman," he said to himself. "For the right price, he will sell us the land where the magical walnut tree grows."

That evening, the sawmill owner visited the woodsman. "You have struggled for many years to feed your family, haven't you, my friend?" he began, with a smile that was a little too big. When the woodsman nodded, he continued. "I want to make a deal with you. I want to buy your land. With the money I will pay you, you will never have to worry again about caring for your family."

"Oh, no," said the woodsman. "This land belonged to my father and my grandfather. It will belong to my children after me. I could never sell this land. I have everything I could possibly want here. I am happy. Life is good for us."

The sawmill owner argued with the woodsman for a long time. He offered more and more money. Still the woodsman refused to sell his land. Finally, the sawmill owner left in a whirlwind of anger.

For days, the owner of the sawmill could think of nothing but the woodsman's small forest and its magical walnut tree. He wanted it so badly he could not eat or drink.

When his wife discovered what was troubling him, she said, "Why don't you just take some walnuts? Go to the forest tonight and bring home a big basket full. And stop feeling sorry for yourself. You are an important man. Don't let that little woodsman stand in your way."

So that very night, the sawmill owner and his son stole into the woodsman's forest to gather some walnuts. When they found the walnut tree in the darkness, they both grabbed hold and shook with all their might. Walnuts by the dozens rained to the ground. They shook and shook until no more walnuts fell. Then they gathered them into baskets and hurried home.

The owner's wife was already in bed when they returned. They made so much noise laughing and congratulating each other about their success that she nearly threw a chair at them.

When they had carried the baskets inside, they excitedly spread the walnuts on the kitchen floor. Then they sat down to see what would happen. They waited and waited, but nothing happened. Finally, they became bored and went to bed.

As you can see, the sawmill owner and his son were both ignorant of the ways of fairies. The twenty-eighth edition of the *Encyclopedia of Fairies,* volume 12, page 536, states clearly that fairies will not come out of walnut shells so long as there are people around. (Acorns are an entirely different story, as everyone knows). As soon as people are in bed, though, fairies burst out of walnuts like popcorn. No sooner had the sawmill owner and his son fallen asleep than the walnuts began to shake and spin and open. Dozens of fairies flew out into the quiet house.

Perhaps you have noticed something about children. While it is not terribly difficult to get one child to do housework, it is very hard to get several children to do housework at the same time. Children begin washing dishes or making

beds, and before long they are splashing water on each other or having a pillow fight.

Now, most authorities will tell you that fairies are a lot like children. One or two fairies are a lot of help around the house. When you get a few, and especially when you get dozens and dozens, they start to act silly and play instead of working. And fairies can play rough.

That is why the sawmill owner, his wife, and his son were awakened in the middle of the night by the sound of clanging pots, splintering wood, and shattering glass. In horror, they rushed to the kitchen to find fairies flitting here and there, smashing chairs against the wall, playing sword fight with the kitchen utensils, and tossing the best dishes through the windows.

Frantically, the sawmill owner ran through the kitchen, chasing the fairies this way and that. Of course, he did not catch them. When was the last time *you* caught a fairy?

When one of the fairies saw he was being chased, he sped into the dining room while several others scooted a chair into the doorway. Before he knew what happened, the sawmill owner had tripped over the chair and was flying toward the dining room table. He landed with a tremendous crash.

After he struggled to his feet, the fairies began to chase him. Normally, fairies are afraid of people, which is why you and I do not see them very often. But when you get a group of them together, and when they have begun to have some fun, they get bolder. These fairies were having so much fun and had become so bold that one flew up to pull the sawmill owner's hair, another tripped him as he stumbled backward, another pulled at his nightshirt.

To make matters even worse, some of the fairies escaped through the broken windows and were making havoc of the

67

sawmill. Through the night, one could hear crashing and banging as the sawmill was taken apart piece by piece.

When morning came, the whole town gathered at the sawmill to survey the damage. Everything was destroyed. The sawmill owner told everyone that a pack of wild dogs had gotten loose in his house. No one believed that story, so he said that it was really a herd of cattle that had strayed from their farm. When no one believed that, he just stopped trying to explain what had happened.

Later that day, the woodsman visited the sawmill owner. "I have a deal for you," he said. "I have saved some money from selling vegetables in town. I would like to buy your sawmill and house from you. I have saved enough to fix them so they will be good as new." Since the sawmill owner had lost everything, and since his home insurance had no provisions for damage done by fairies, he could do nothing but agree.

So, the woodsman bought the sawmill and repaired it. Before long, woodsmen were bringing trees from miles away because he always paid them a fair price. He worked hard and lived prosperously and happily for the rest of his life.

And, though he never again needed a magical walnut, the woodsman always made sure that the polite squirrel's tree was not cut down.

MORAL

Dishonest money dwindles away, but he who
gathers money little by little makes it grow.
(Prov. 13:11, NIV)

Chapter VIII

ivy and the prince

nce upon a time, there was a beautiful young woman named Ivy. Ivy loved to walk through the forest, smelling the flowers, singing with the birds, chasing the rabbits as her long golden hair fluttered in the wind like a banner. She thought of the forest as her very own garden.

Ivy's father had told her that she could explore the forest as much as she wished. "Only do not pass through the thicket of briars at the center of the forest," he warned her. "On the other side, there are many dangers. If you go through the briars, you will surely die."

Ivy happily obeyed her father, since there was much to see on her side of the briar thicket.

One day, when she began to chase a rabbit, the rabbit did not run away. Instead, he turned and looked directly at her. Then he spoke.

"I have often seen you in the forest," he said. "You love the forest very much, don't you?"

Though surprised to come across a talking rabbit, Ivy answered, "Oh, yes, I love the forest more than anything."

"I have noticed, though," the rabbit continued, "that you stay on this side of the forest and never go past the briar thicket."

"My father told me that it was very dangerous on the other side and that I should never pass through the thicket. He said if I passed through the thicket something horrible would happen and I would die."

The rabbit nodded. He seemed sad.

"What is wrong?" Ivy asked, feeling sorry for the sad little rabbit.

"I am thinking of all that you are missing because you may not go to the other side. There are many flowers there that do not grow here, and many animals to play with that do not run on this side. The birds sing so sweetly there. They are a delight to the ears. If only you could go to the other side, it would bring you such pleasure."

The rabbit stopped for a moment, and then added, "There is one way. Oh no, I should not mention it."

"What?"

"I should say nothing more." The rabbit began to hop away.

"Oh, please, tell me. Please."

The rabbit stopped. "I should not say anything. But. You said your father will not let you pass *through* the briar thicket?"

"Yes."

"Did you know there is a way *around* the thicket? Perhaps you could follow me along that path. You could go to the other side without disobeying your father."

Ivy frowned. The rabbit's words sounded like something her logic teacher might have said, and she had never quite trusted him.

70

"If you do not want to follow me, I understand," the rabbit said, and he began to hop off again. "You should not go on the other side. Not if your father forbids it. Not if you don't want to."

"Oh, but I do. I do." Ivy frowned again, stamped her foot, crossed her arms, uncrossed them, and stood thinking. After a moment, she shouted after him, "I had to think about it. Of course I will follow you. Let's go."

The rabbit led her round and round among the tall pine trees until they came to the edge of the thicket. There Ivy could see colorful birds she had never imagined darting through the air, singing ever so sweetly. White and yellow and violet and scarlet flowers covered a hillside. Cuddly animals rolled and played in the thick grass.

The beauty of the world beyond the thicket so overwhelmed her that she ran past the rabbit to the other side.

Ivy had no sooner stepped past the briar thicket than the birds stopped singing. The flowers drooped and turned brown. The cuddly animals disappeared. She turned to ask the rabbit what had happened, but it was no rabbit behind her. Where the rabbit had been there was now a terrifying and dreadful dragon, with iron teeth and horrible sharp horns.

Quickly she tried to run but fell. In terror, she saw the dragon raise a claw to strike her. But then she saw another face, the handsome face of a young man. A golden sword flashed, cleaving dragon's head. That was the last thing she saw.

After making certain the dragon was dead, the young man looked down at the beautiful Ivy and loved her with all his heart. He raised her head and kissed her. Ivy felt his

71

warm breath on her cheek and his strong arm around her shoulder.

Then as the young man took a golden chain, thin and fine as a hair, and tied it among Ivy's tresses. Bending down, he whispered, "If ever you need me, untie this chain. I will come. I will come again." But his words came too late. Ivy had already fainted away and did not hear his promise.

When Ivy awoke, she was lying in bed at home. Her father was holding her hand.

"Where is he?" she asked.

"Who?"

"The young man with the golden sword. He saved me from that terrible dragon." She shuddered.

"The prince has gone to his home. He lives in a golden castle in the clouds."

"When is he coming back?"

"No one knows for sure," her father said quietly. "Now, you need to rest. When you have regained your strength, I want to talk about your disobedience."

"Oh, father, I am so sorry. Please forgive me. I will never do it again. Never."

"You are forgiven. But you must rest. There will be time to talk later."

The next day Ivy had a fever. Her face was flushed, and her left side ached. A doctor was called, but he could find nothing wrong. "Give her a few more days rest, and she will be fine," the doctor said.

A few days passed, but Ivy was not fine. Her fever grew worse, as if she were lit by an inner flame. The pain in her heart did not go away. She ate little and barely slept. Whenever she closed her eyes, she could see only the face of the young prince who had saved her. She remembered how closely he had held her, she felt his breath on her cheek, and her mind filled with the strange terror of love.

But all the while she knew nothing of the golden chain tied in her golden hair. She had not heard the promise of the prince from the castle in the clouds.

Whenever she awoke, she spoke of him. One night, she cried out in her sleep, "We must have lamp oil!"

"We must have what?" her father asked, looking up from a book.

"Lamp oil! Lamp oil! The house must be lighted when he returns!" Ivy sat up in bed, still asleep though her eyes were wide open. "We must be ready for him! We cannot let him surprise us!"

"Yes, yes. I will make sure that we have plenty of oil." Her father laid her down. She closed her eyes and whispered, "Come, my lord. Come quickly." Soon she was sleeping again.

Another day, she was sitting in bed staring at the plate of food on her lap, when without warning she jumped up and ran toward the door, scattering food and drink everywhere.

"Ivy!" her father cried, wiping a stain from his shirt.

"He's at the door." Ivy's eyes were wide with fright.

"Who is at the door?"

"The prince from the castle in the clouds! He has returned for me! I heard him at my door! His hand was in the keyhole! He was trying to open my door!"

"I heard nothing," her father assured her. "There is no one at your door."

"Please, father, open it and see."

Her father opened the door and looked out. "No one," he said, shutting the door quietly.

73

"I was sure he was there." She was trembling with cold and fever. "Oh, my heart is burning." She turned her thin face toward her father. "Please, father. Promise me you will search for him and tell him how I love him, and how I will die if he does not come to me. Please ask him to return."

"I promise."

The very next day, her father put Ivy in the care of a nurse and left to search for the prince. While he was gone, Ivy's fever worsened, as did the pain in her heart. She refused to eat and wasted away to nothing.

When her father returned and saw Ivy lying on the bed, he thought she was dead. In the light of the oil lamps, her skin looked thin as paper. Her body was as frail as a doll's. Gently he touched her hand, and her eyes quickly opened.

"Father," Ivy whispered. "Did you find him?"

Her father was crying. "I searched everywhere. I asked everyone I knew, everyone I met. But I could not find him. They asked me why I was searching for him. They told me he is not here, that he has gone back to his castle in the sky. I am so sorry."

Ivy's eyes closed. A tear rolled down her face onto the pillow. As her father stroked her hair, he felt something tangled there. Curious, he looked closer and discovered a golden chain, as thin and fine as a hair. He untied it and held it up to the light.

Suddenly the young prince burst through the door. At first, Ivy's father thought he was a thief. He was so startled he fell over backwards, and another of Ivy's uneaten dinners splattered on him. The prince bent over at Ivy's side, touched her hand, and breathed on her cheek. "My dearest, arise," he said in a gently commanding voice.

For a moment, Ivy did not move. Her father watched breathlessly, ignoring for the moment the stains on his new shirt. He saw her hand tighten on the prince's. He saw her lips move in a silent prayer of thanks. Her tear-filled eyes opened and she saw her prince face to face. Her heart broke with pain and joy and the terror of love.

"My lord. What I am to you? I am only a skeleton," Ivy whispered.

"You are better than ten men to me," said the prince.

Weak as she was, Ivy sat up and held him, as her tears flowed. And her fever left her that very hour.

Soon after, Ivy married the prince and they went to live in his golden castle in the clouds. There, he gave her a garden for her very own. It was filled with flowers, birds, and animals. But there was no more briar thicket.

Ivy and her husband had many beautiful children, and they lived happily ever after.

MORAL

Hope deferred makes the heart sick,
but desire fulfilled is a tree of life.
(Prov. 13:12)

Chapter IX

BLIND STRANGER

t was twilight on the winter night when he came down into the mountain village, dressed all in black, eyes covered with a dark bandage. In his hand was a long white cane whose handle was coiled like a serpent. He tapped the cane lightly on the street as he walked.

Villagers peered through the windows of their stone houses or opened their doors a crack to look at the stranger. His feet seemed to them to slither over the cobblestones as he shuffled past.

One little boy, looking down from his bedroom, called loudly, "Mama, why does he have that bandage on his face?" In a stern whisper, his mother told him the man was blind and it was not polite to talk about it.

The stranger in black stopped at four houses to ask lodging for the night. At the first three houses, no one answered his knock. At the fourth house, he was greeted by a harsh voice that said, "Go away. We don't want you."

Tapping his cane, the stranger continued to the middle of the village. At the village square he stopped, cocked his head to the side, and listened. Following the sounds of laughter, he walked to the inn to ask for a room. As he walked in, the people inside stopped eating and drinking and fell silent.

The innkeeper made an ugly face. "No rooms left," he grunted. "You could stay out in the room over the shed. It is dry. You can have some straw for a bed. It will be comfortable enough—for you," he sneered.

The stranger nodded, and the people of the inn watched as the innkeeper led him out a side door toward the shed.

The mayor, who was eating with the sheriff, was the first to break the silence. "I don't like strangers in my town. And I don't like him. Blind people aren't like us, you know."

"Say, did you see that cane? It looked like a snake!" the innkeeper said when he returned.

"We'll have to keep our eye on him," the mayor muttered, nodding.

The next day, however, everything was normal as villagers returned to their work. Each day was pretty much the same in that small village in the mountains. Grownups worked together from sunrise to sunset, while their children learned lessons in the whitewashed schoolhouse. In the evening, they ate a hearty dinner, played or sang around the fire until bedtime, and slept soundly in the cold winter night.

For his part, the stranger stayed in the shed beside the inn most of the time. Each evening, he would enter the inn, eat a thin bowl of soup for supper, walk once around the village square, and return to the shed. Other than that, the villagers almost never saw him. No one knew what he did in the room above the shed all day, and before long no one cared to know.

Several months later, a terrible storm broke out on the mountain. Great boulders of hail fell from the black clouds. Lightning struck the steeple of the church, and the roof caught fire. Before it could be stopped, the fire had leaped to the roof of a nearby home, then another and another. By the time the villagers were able to put out the fire, a third of the houses were destroyed.

A town meeting was held the next day in the square. The priest encouraged the assembled villagers. "We have survived disasters before, and with God's help we can survive this too. God has given a chance to show our love for one another. Let us work together and rebuild our town."

Most of the villagers were cheered by the priest's words. But the mayor had never liked the priest, because before him the mayor felt like a sinner. While the priest spoke, the mayor whispered to the sheriff and cast suspicious glances toward the shed next to the inn.

Only a week later, a disease struck the villagers' animals, which they pastured in the valley below. All over the valley, cows, sheep, and goats coughed up blood and fell over dead. By the end of a week, a third of the animals had died. The river rippling through the valley turned red with their blood.

Another town meeting was hastily called. The priest again spoke to the crowd. He urged them to fast and pray, to repent and humble themselves. He assured them of God's mercy and justice and led them in a hymn of praise.

With the last chord of the hymn still hanging on the mountain air, the mayor stepped to the front of the crowd and motioned for silence.

"We all thank you, Father, for your words of comfort," he said with a broad smile. "But we need more than comfort. We need a solution. To arrive at a solution, we need to understand the problem."

The villagers listened intently.

"Think carefully now," the mayor continued. "When did these terrible plagues begin? And what else happened about the same time?"

Whispers, some of them bitter, rippled through the crowd.

"That's right," said the mayor. "That stranger, that blind stranger, came into our village only a short while before the fire! And now our animals are dying. Tell me, neighbors, do you think that was a coincidence?"

From the back of the crowd someone who sounded a lot like the sheriff shouted very loudly, "NO!" Some in the crowd nodded vigorously. Others looked puzzled.

The village smithy raised his hand to speak. "I don't know about the rest of you. But I haven't seen that stranger do anything wrong. Why, just the other day, he stopped to talk to my little girl on one of his walks. He asked her age and what size clothes she wears. He was trying to get an idea of how big she is, since he can't see and all. She said he seemed real nice." Others murmured that the same thing had happened to their children.

The mayor interrupted before the smithy could finish. "He has been talking to our sons and daughters? And you think that's 'nice,' do you? Well, I will tell you what I think. I think he's planning to harm them. That is what I think."

Several voices shouted their agreement. The smithy tried to speak again, but the voices got louder. Confused, then angry, he looked around at the crowd and sat down.

The priest stood again, trying to be heard. "Come, my children," he said when the shouting stopped. "You are suspicious for nothing. This stranger has nothing to do with the evil things that have been happening. I have talked with him many times and can tell you he is a kind and generous man.

Perhaps these things have happened because we have not treated him well. We have not shown him hospitality. He came to us, and we have not received him."

"Aha!" the mayor's voice boomed out. "*You* have gotten to know him? And what have you two been planning together?"

The mayor had gone too far this time. Suspicious though the villagers were, the priest had been their faithful friend and shepherd for longer than most could remember. If anyone could be trusted, surely it was he.

Realizing the crowd had turned against him, the mayor snorted loudly and walked away, shouting, "We shall see."

The next months were quiet. The last cold of the mountain winter melted into spring. The villagers went back to work and play and rest and worship. As the weather warmed, the church and the burned houses were rebuilt. Healthy goats, sheep, and cattle were born. The troubles of the past began to seem far away.

The calm was broken one spring afternoon by a scream. The villagers stopped what they were doing and looked in the direction of the inn. There they saw the innkeeper's wife running around the town square wildly waving her arms. Soon everyone had gathered around her.

Between sobs, she tried to explain. "She's gone. My daughter. I put her down for a nap. And now she's gone."

Immediately, the villagers spread out to search for the little lost girl. They searched every street and alley, every store, every house, every garden. But the innkeeper's daughter could not be found.

Villager after villager returned from the search with bad news. As the mob grew, the mayor climbed the inn's porch and began to speak.

"Do you remember what I told you? Didn't I tell you that our children would be harmed?" The mob remembered.

The mayor continued, "I have been talking with the innkeeper's wife. I think you will be interested in what she told me. Yesterday she saw her daughter with—guess who? Our blind stranger!" The mob gasped as one man. "And now her daughter is gone! How long will we let this go on?"

"No more!" the mob shouted. "Bring him down! Let's stop this now!"

The mayor motioned to the sheriff, who took two men and ran into shed. A few minutes later they returned dragging the blind stranger. At the sight of his black clothes and serpent-like cane, the mob's shouts grew louder.

"We found him knitting," the sheriff announced.

"Knitting!" cried the mayor. "Knitting! Do you know what kind of men knit? Ask the schoolteacher! Sorcerers, magicians, and witches knit, isn't that right?" The teacher nodded wisely. "Why, the stranger must be a conjurer, a witch, as well as a stealer of children."

"Drive out the witch!" the mob screamed.

The priest had climbed the steps, trying desperately to speak. "Please, please! Stop this madness!" he pleaded.

"Drive out the witch! Drive out the witch!" the crowd chanted.

"Why?" screamed the priest. "What evil has he done?"

But they shouted all the more, "Drive out the witch! Drive out the witch!"

The priest turned to the judge, who had come from working in his garden. "Can't you stop this?" the priest asked.

Raising his hands in a shrug, the judge answered, "I wash my hands of the matter."

The mob began to shout again. With an effort, the priest quieted them. "I tell you, this man is innocent of all wrong," he said. "And if you continue to demand that he leave our village, I will go with him."

At this, the mob became silent and uncomfortable. They thought of the children the priest had baptized, of the boys and girls he had taught, of the widows and orphans he had comforted. They thought of his preaching and breaking bread. How could they live without their priest?

The mayor spoke again. "My friends, I know how much you love our priest. But can you trust a priest who would defend a sorcerer? Perhaps the priest too is a child-snatcher! Perhaps we would all be better off without him as well."

From the back of the mob, someone cried out, "Drive out the witch! Drive out the witch!" Quietly at first, then louder and louder, the mob joined in the chant.

"I warn you, if I leave today, I will never return!" the priest shouted over the din.

"Drive out the priest! Drive out the priest!" the mob answered.

Sadly, the priest walked down the steps of the inn, the blind stranger beside him. The people parted and the two passed through. As they walked through the mob, the smithy's daughter spat on them.

Toward the edge of the village, the road became rockier, and the priest held the stranger's arm to steady him, as they went past the last houses. Soon, the two figures had disappeared around a turn of the mountain path.

Driven by their anger, the crowd hurried to the blind stranger's room. There as they searched through the room above the shed, the villagers found dozens of knitted children's sweaters and caps, in all sizes and colors.

The innkeeper's daughter was found later that day. She had sneaked from her room into the barn next door and fallen behind a haystack. Except for an ugly bruise on her head and a twisted knee, she was fine.

Forty days after the priest and the blind stranger left, a rock slide buried the entire village. Not one stone was left upon another, which was not torn down.

MORAL

He who gives an answer before he hears,
it is folly and shame to him.
(Prov. 18:13)

85

Chapter X

CHE FRAGRANT GARDEN

nce upon a time, there was a man who had three sons. When they grew up, he gave each a garden to dress and keep for himself.

The first son, whose name was Adam, was very lazy. When his father gave him his garden, he did no work at all. He did not tend the flowers or weed the vegetables, and soon the flowers were dying and the vegetables were rotting on the vine. The wind blew across his garden, and carried the smell of rotting flowers and vegetables throughout the town.

One day, a man appeared at Adam's garden. "I am an inspector from the Ministry of Nasty Smells," he said, wrinkling his nose in disgust. "We have had some complaints about your garden." This was a town, you can see, that took its gardening seriously.

"What kind of complaints?" Adam asked, yawning as if he were bored. Lazy people, as you may know, are bored most of the time, and bored people are usually lazy too.

"There are complaints that the smells from your garden are spreading throughout the town. The mayor has asked me to tell you to plow up your garden and move somewhere else, immediately," said the inspector, whose name was Felix.

Even Adam realized he had no choice about the matter now. But not wishing to lose everything, Adam decided to gather what he could to sell in the town market. The next morning, he was in the town square with a cart full of limp celery, brown lettuce, wrinkled tomatoes, and other foods that were so unappetizing it would make you sick if I were to describe them.

A few people stopped to glance into Adam's cart, but after a quick look they rushed on looking rather green themselves—more green, in fact, than Adam's vegetables were. At mid-morning, a man walked up and introduced himself.

"I am an inspector from the Ministry for the Elimination of Yucky Food," he said. "We have had some complaints about the food you are offering for sale."

"Complaints? What kind of complaints?" Adam asked in surprise. Like many lazy people, the first son was none too bright.

"Why, your food. It is absolutely—what is the right word? Why, it is yucky," said the inspector, whose name was Festus. "The mayor has told me that you cannot sell your food here anymore."

So Adam pulled his cart out of town and was never heard from again.

The second of the man's three sons, whose name was Jacob, was very different from the first. He was not lazy at all. Instead, he was a very hard worker. Jacob's garden was filled with bright fragrant roses, sunshiny daffodils, petunias of every color, and lilac that smelled better than the perfumes of Arabia, which smell awfully good. Jacob worked to produce the best vegetables, plump tomatoes, crisp lettuce and celery, herbs, beans, peas, and I don't know what else. Everyone who passed by agreed Jacob's was the most beautiful garden they had ever seen.

But, although he was not lazy, Jacob was very greedy. He took no joy in his work, but instead he labored from sunrise to sunset only so he could sell his flowers and vegetables at the highest prices. Because he was so very greedy, two things made him very angry. When the wind blew across his garden, it spread the delightful fragrances of his flowers throughout the town. Everyone breathed deeply of the sweet smells—without paying anything! Also townspeople enjoyed walking past his garden to look at his flowers. On Sundays, it seemed that the whole town came for a look.

No one will buy my flowers, Jacob thought angrily, if they can smell them and look at them for nothing. He fumed and fussed about this for days, and finally he decided upon a plan. The next day, he bought the best building materials and in a few days had erected a dome that covered his entire garden. "No one will get another free look at my flowers! And the wind will not be able to carry their fragrance to the townspeople for nothing!" he said in satisfaction.

Like most greedy people, Jacob was none too bright. For of course, if you build a dome over it, your garden will not get the sun and rain it needs to grow. After Jacob built the dome, the wind did not carry the flowers' fragrance around town, but neither did it bring the fresh air that the plants needed to live. Within a few weeks, Jacob's flowers were dying, and the vegetables were rotting on their stems. Before long, the men from the Ministry of Nasty Smells and the Ministry for the Elimination of Yucky Food had asked the second son to leave town.

89

That left only the last son, whose name was Paul. Paul was not at all like Adam, and even less like Jacob. He was neither lazy nor greedy. He was simply good. He loved to dig deep into the dirt, to watch the first sprouts fight their way toward the sun, to wait patiently while vegetables ripened through various shades of green, orange, and red.

When the wind carried the fragrances of his flowers throughout town, Paul did not become angry. He wanted to share his garden with everyone, near and far. When townspeople walked by his garden on Sundays to glimpse his flowers, he invited them in and gave them a tour, teaching all he knew about even the smallest blossom. Paul did not keep his vegetables to himself but sold the best of them in the town square. Everyone agreed that Paul had the loveliest flowers and the tastiest vegetables of all.

Well, not exactly everyone. One day two men visited Paul's garden. "I am an inspector from the Ministry of Nasty Smells," Felix said with a bow. "We have had some complaints about your garden."

Paul was puzzled. "What kind of complaints?"

"It seems that one of your neighbors has complained about the nasty smells the wind blows from your garden."

"But there are no nasty smells from my garden. The fragrances of my garden are wonderful. Here, smell this yourself," he said as he handed Felix a pink rose.

Sighing deeply, Felix closed his eyes in delight, which gave the second man, who, as you might have guessed, was Festus, a chance to speak. "I am an inspector from the Ministry for the Elimination of Yucky Food. There has been a complaint about the vegetables you have been selling in the town square," Festus said. "Someone, it appears, has become ill after eating one of your tomatoes. He has filed a complaint that your tomatoes are, what shall I say? Yucky."

Paul was stupefied, as I am sure you would be in the same circumstances. "But I sell only my very best vegetables in the square. They are delicious, and all are healthy. Here, try one for yourself."

When Festus bit into the tomato, a wave of juice splashed into his mouth. "Absolutely delicious," he said, wiping his mouth with a white handkerchief. "Heavenly, really."

The inspector from the Ministry of Nasty Smells had been silent for a few moments, standing with the rose pressed against his cheek, eyes closed in rapture, a serene smile on his face. When Festus spoke, Felix started as if he were waking from a dream, and his smile disappeared. "I am sorry," he said. "But we must investigate every complaint to its fullest. You must come with us."

Still puzzled, Paul followed the inspectors to the town hall and into the large room where the mayor was holding court. Already seated at the front was the neighbor who had made the complaints. Paul knew him well. His name was Judah, and he had often spread falsehoods about Paul's garden. The mayor, whose name, in case you were wondering, was Harold, called everyone to attention.

"Court is now in session. The first case comes jointly from the Ministry of Nasty Smells and the Ministry for the Elimination of Yucky Food. It seems that some quite deathly odors have been coming from your garden and that one of your tomatoes made a buyer sick," Harold said, nodding in Paul's direction. "Who makes this accusation?"

"I do, Your Honor," Judah said as he stood up. "It is true. The smells from his garden are more than nasty. They are evil. It is a fragrance of death, I tell you, and it is about

91

to kill me. And that tomato I bought. It was rotten from skin to core. I almost died when I ate it. I want him driven from his garden forever."

The mayor looked at Paul. "What do you have to say for yourself?"

Paul produced a bouquet of flowers and two tomatoes from a basket and placed them before Mayor Harold. "This is my only defense," he said. "May I ask a few questions of my accuser?"

Mayor Harold's eyes had closed as he buried his nose into the bouquet, and now he started as if he were waking from a dream. "Why, yes. That is your right." He picked up a tomato and bit into it. A gush of juice drenched his desk.

Paul stood before his accuser. "Tell me, Judah, do you have a garden yourself?"

"That has nothing to do with anything! Tell him he cannot ask me that kind of question!" Judah shouted at the mayor.

Mayor Harold was mopping tomato juice from the pages of a thick book. "Oh, I am afraid you are wrong. He can ask such questions as much as he wishes. And you must answer." He took another bite of the tomato.

"Well, yes," the neighbor said at last.

"May we see some of your flowers?" Paul asked.

"That is not fair," Judah shouted again. "My flowers are not making those deathly smells. His are! His are!"

"Nonetheless," the mayor answered, trying to remain dignified while an avalanche of tomato seeds slid down his chin, "you must do as he asks. Produce some of your own flowers."

Judah left the courtroom and returned with a bouquet of faded violets and tiny roses.

"Tell me," said the last son. "Do you sell any of your flowers?"

Judah exploded in rage. "I used to! I did until you started your garden! I used to have the most fragrant garden in town! Then you pushed in here, and everyone is talking about how wonderful your flowers smell, and how good your vegetables are, and now everyone just forgot about me and stopped buying my fruit! It's not fair! It's not fair!"

Paul walked to a chair and sat down. "Mayor Harold," he said quietly. "I have no more to say."

Mayor Harold had by this time regained his composure, and, feeling quite comfortable after a delicious tomato, was ready to give his verdict. "It is clear that you have made this accusation from envy," he said to Judah in a stern, mayoral voice. "Because the fragrance from your flowers was no longer the most beautiful fragrance, you have tried to destroy the work of this fine young man. I find no fault in him.

"As for you, Judah. You were given the choicest land by your own father. For a short time, your garden produced wonderful flowers and vegetables. You even, if I recall, had a vineyard, and your grapes were delicious. But you neglected your duties, and now it is a very poor excuse for a garden. And because you have made a false accusation, my sentence is that your garden shall be taken from you and given to Paul, who will certainly use it better than you have. And you," he said to Judah, "shall leave this town and never return. That is my decision."

Mayor Harold raised his gavel to strike on his desk, but being so very dignified, he did not notice the second tomato. Some say they are still cleaning the courtroom to this day, but I do not quite believe that.

From that day on, Paul lived happily ever after, growing vegetables to sell and flowers whose pleasant fragrances the wind carried to the ends of the earth.

MORAL

A false witness will not go unpunished,
and he who tells lies will not escape.
(Prov. 19:5)

Chapter XI

The Monster's House

nce upon a time, there was a land far, far away where all the people lived in terror of a great monster. This monster dwelt on a high mountain that was always covered with a thick cloud.

No one had seen the monster at any time. It was said that at night the cloud would light up like a bonfire, and the monster would stalk the land, kidnapping anyone it found and carrying him away to its mountain home. Nearly every family had lost a father or mother, a son or daughter. Sometimes entire families would suddenly turn up missing, and everyone would know exactly what had happened even without saying it.

Some said the monster was a giant hairy man, taller than a tree, with one eye in the middle of his forehead and another in the middle of his chest, and perhaps one on each knee. Others said it was a dragon, with as many legs as a centipede and ten horns sprouting from three heads. Still others believed that the monster could change shape at will, appearing now with the face of an ox, now with the face of an eagle or lion, now with the face of a man. But no one really knew what the monster looked like, since no one had ever seen it—at least, no one who had lived to tell about it.

All the knights and warriors of the land had gone to battle the monster, but none returned. As soon as they touched
the mountain, it seemed, they were doomed. When search
parties were sent to find them, they discovered no clues to
tell them what had happened.

In the end, there were no warriors left. Men who were
less well trained in the ways of war began to venture off,
hoping to save the land from the monster and to make a
name for themselves. Farmers, a woodcutter, some of the
craftsmen from the surrounding villages, they all climbed the
mountain. Like the warriors, they never came back.

By the small stream that flowed at the foot of the monster's mountain lived a man named Zeke with his wife and
four children. Zeke knew of the monster and had heard all
the stories. He did not believe any of them. Besides, Zeke
believed in living and letting live. As long as the monster left
him and his family alone, Zeke never took time to think
about it, much less to go off adventuring to destroy the monster.

That all changed one morning when Zeke awoke to find
his house empty. His wife and children had been stolen quietly in the night. Then and there, Zeke resolved that, come
what may, he would do everything in his power to rescue
them from the monster. That very night, he packed a bag
with food and a bread knife, which was the nearest thing to
a weapon he could find, and started up the mountain. Above
him he saw the thick cloud, glowing red and orange against
the black night sky.

It took most of the night to climb to the peak. At dawn,
Zeke pulled himself up onto a plateau at the top of the
mountain. Through swirling clouds, he saw an odd white
building. Hiding as best he could behind small bushes and

gnarled mountain trees, he made his way toward the building, which he was certain was the monster's palace.

A high wall encircled the courtyard of the palace, but Zeke was able to find a small opening to peek through. In the growing morning light, the house looked even stranger than it had in the shadows of dawn, like something from a half-remembered dream. Its size was enormous, almost too big to sit on a mountain top, big enough, it seemed to Zeke, to fill the whole earth.

The house was unfinished. Towers poked up here and there for no apparent reason, some stretching high into the sky, others seemingly abandoned shortly after they were begun. The wall varied in height, with large gaps all around.

The house was made of pure white brick, but the bricks were like nothing Zeke had ever seen. They were of irregular size and shape, so that Zeke, though he knew something about buildings, could not understand how the house held together. It teetered back and forth, threatening each moment to collapse into a heap. Yet, supported by some unseen power, it never fell.

More strangely even than this, it seemed to Zeke that each brick of the house was in constant motion. At first, he was certain the morning light and the misty clouds were playing tricks with his eyes. The more he looked, the more convinced Zeke became that each brick was alive—and breathing!

As Zeke stared in wonder at the house, a door opened and five figures stepped into the court. To his horror, Zeke recognized them as his wife and children. A sixth figure, shrouded in dark robes, followed them. When they reached the center of the yard, Zeke's wife and children stopped and turned to face the mysterious robed figure, who said something Zeke could not hear.

From a large basin, the man in dark robes drew some water and poured it over Zeke's wife and children. Then, the figure handed something to each and pointed toward a doorway. They disappeared and returned a few moments later wearing long robes as white as snow. The dark figure pulled a small golden pitcher from somewhere in the folds of his robe, and, as Zeke's family knelt before him, he poured a thick sparkling liquid on their heads.

Zeke had at first been frightened, but now he was confused. "They seem to be going along with this! They must be enchanted," he thought grimly. If that were true, there was no hope, for Zeke knew he was no match for a wizard.

While these thoughts flooded his mind, Zeke's wife and children lay down in narrow metal boxes, stretching out as if in coffins. When they were still, the robed figure walked to the far end of the court and grasped a knot of ropes. As he pulled the ropes, the metal boxes rose higher and higher into the air. Zeke saw the boxes were hanging high over a huge, sharp rock.

"If they fall on that rock, they will be broken to pieces," Zeke said to himself. "I have seen enough of this." Boldly pulling his bread knife from his pack, he climbed the wall. As he reached the top, the robed figure was about to let the boxes fall. "Stop!" Zeke shouted. "Don't let them fall! You'll kill them!"

Suspended above the rock in their metal coffins, Zeke's wife and children sat up and looked. The robed figure spun around, surprised by Zeke's cry. As he turned, his hood fell back, revealing a head of white hair and a white beard framing a face bronzed by the sun. His eyes blazed at Zeke, but he began to lower the coffins to the ground.

"Stop!" Zeke cried again as he leaped down into the courtyard. "I am come to rescue you! Let's go home," he cried to his family. "Before the monster finds us!"

By this time, the boxes were only a few feet above the ground, and Zeke's wife jumped out and threw herself into Zeke's arms. "Zeke," she cried. "I was hoping you would be summoned too. I am so happy you are here."

"Summoned? Happy? What do you mean? I was not summoned. I came to rescue you. And you, you were kidnapped, weren't you?"

"Oh no!" she said, laughing. "We came up the mountain freely. Ever since my friends came up, I have wanted to come. You remember Sarah and Rebecca, don't you? They are here too." As she said this, she waved her hand toward the east wall of the house, and for a moment Zeke thought some of the white bricks looked oddly familiar. One seemed to smile kindly at him.

Zeke shook his head and rubbed his eyes. "Darling, you have been enchanted by this, this wizard here! And I am becoming enchanted too! Come with me now, while we still can! Let's go back home!"

"But I do not want to go home. And besides, I cannot go home. I have been summoned, and so have our children. We cannot refuse after we have been summoned. This is our home now."

The bearded man in dark robes had come close and now interrupted. "Perhaps I can explain," he said. His voice resounded like a distant waterfall.

"Who are you? The monster's assistant? Where is the master of the house?" Zeke brandished his bread knife threateningly in front of the old man's face. "Don't come a step closer," he said, vainly hoping his voice sounded more fierce than fearful. In spite of himself, Zeke was fascinated by the old man, whose voice was like that of a dear friend whose memory Zeke had, for some awful reason, tried to erase from his mind.

The old man's face softened into a smile. "You are very mistaken. There is no monster. I myself am the master of the house."

Zeke sat down on the ground, his head spinning. "Maybe you should explain," he said, still careful to keep the sharp end of the bread knife pointed toward the old man.

"I am the king of this land," the old man began. "All the people are my subjects, though many do not know me. Others I choose and summon to my mountain, so that these, at least, will know their king. It is a great privilege, you see, to be summoned, a privilege I do not extend to all my subjects. Your wife and children were summoned last night, and they have come to stay here forever. And though you did not know it, you also were summoned. That is why you have come."

"But what if I do not want to be summoned? Suppose I like it where I am?" To Zeke, the old man was more terrifying than any monster, though his voice and manner were gentle.

"It is as your wife said. If one is summoned, he comes. If one is summoned, he wants to come."

Zeke thought a moment. "What were you about to do to them when I climbed over the wall?"

"It is part of the privilege of being on the mountain. Your wife and children—and you yourself—have been chosen to become part of my house. Once you are washed and dressed and anointed, you have to be shaped into bricks. My house is not quite finished, as you can see. I need a great many more bricks."

"Do you have to kill people to make them into bricks?" Zeke asked.

The old man's face became stern. "For those who are summoned, death is but a passage to a life better than you can possibly imagine. They die that they might truly live."

At first, the thought of being turned into a brick had made Zeke sick to his stomach. As the old man spoke, however, by some miracle, that same thought began to fill his heart with a joy he had never known before.

"What about all those warriors who came up here to kill the monster?" Zeke asked, still trying to resist the attraction of the old king and his house of human bricks. By this time, though, he was using the bread knife to cut slices of bread for himself and his family.

"They found no monster, I am afraid," the king said, still stern. "They found only me. Some of them were summoned, and they are now bricks in my house. Some of them wanted only to kill and destroy, and those lie crushed beneath the great rock in the courtyard. Everyone who comes to the mountain faces one of two ends: Either he falls on the rock and becomes a brick in my house, or the rock falls on him and he is crushed to dust. There is no third choice."

Zeke's wife and children looked at him expectantly. "Well?" they said finally.

"Well, what?"

"Are you staying?"

Zeke shook his head and laughed because there was nothing else to do but laugh. It did not begin as a joyful laugh, but when he stopped laughing he was wildly happy. "I do

103

not seem to have any choice. I am staying one way or the other. And becoming a brick is a far sight better than becoming dust."

While his wife and children looked on, the king led Zeke to the middle of the court, where he was washed, dressed in a robe of bright white, and anointed with golden oil. Then he lay down in one of the metal boxes. Before Zeke knew what had happened, his form had changed and he and his wife and children had been fitted into a tower of the king's palace.

Zeke has been a brick in the king's house for many centuries now. New people have been summoned and new bricks added each and every day. Yet even now, the house is unfinished, and it will remain so until the end of time. The king's palace still looks as if it could collapse at any moment, but I, for one, will be very surprised if it ever does.

MORAL

*Man's steps are ordained by the LORD, how
then can man understand His way?*
(Prov. 20:24)

104

Chapter XII

A RELUCTANT RESCUE

nce upon a time, a king named Abraham ruled a beautiful kingdom. His father had been a mighty warrior and had killed many dragons and driven the rest out of the land. Because of his father, Abraham inherited a realm of peace and plenty.

During his second year as king, Abraham married the most beautiful princess in the world, whose name was Sarah, at the most gorgeous wedding there had ever been. They were going to live happily ever after, as kings and queens are said to do at the end of fairy tales.

Or so they thought. In the dark kingdom on the other side of the mountain lived an evil king. He too had wanted to marry princess Sarah, but Abraham had won her heart. As a result, the evil king became angry and bitter, and over the years his bitterness grew and grew.

As often happens to bitter people, the king's appearance began to change. He lost his hair, and his skin hardened into scales. His teeth became sharp as razors, and he grew a tail. His fingers curled into claws, and he walked through his castle on all fours. Batlike wings sprouted from his back. One morning when he looked into the mirror, he had turned completely into a dragon. Still his bitterness burned and bubbled inside him, and great puffs of smoke and fire billowed from his nostrils. (Of course, not all bitter people turn into dragons; but most do.)

All the while, the dragon king planned his revenge. Abraham had taken what he loved, so Abraham would have to pay. Night after night, the dragon crouched on the hill overlooking Abraham's castle, angrily breathing fire and looking for a chance to seize Sarah.

His chance came late on a moonless summer night. Unaware of the danger, King Abraham had taken his best men into the forest for two weeks of hunting. The castle had been left under the protection of the fat butler and the thin cook, who, though sturdy and brave, were no match for a cunning and powerful dragon.

Sarah had just blown out the candle and settled down in bed when something glided through her open window and an awful odor filled her room. A claw closed over her face. She struggled and tried to scream but could not free herself. In the light of the dragon's fiery breath, she saw his horrible grinning face and fainted.

When she awoke, she was in the dungeon of the dragon king's castle. In the dim light, she could see the rats and insects crawling across the floors and walls. The dragon king gazed through the bars of her cell. "Perhaps," he hissed, "perhaps now you shall be my queen and we shall have children of our own."

Terrified by the dragon, and a little sickened by the smell of death on his breath, she fell crying to the floor.

When Abraham returned from the hunt, he found the cook and butler moaning and weeping in the kitchen. All they knew was that Queen Sarah had disappeared mysteriously in the night. Searching his lands, Abraham learned from some of the peasants that a strange creature carrying a heavy burden had been seen flying east on the very night the queen was taken.

As a boy, Abraham had listened eagerly to his father's stories about fighting dragons. But he thought that all the dragons had been killed and that his land was free of danger. He had hoped to live his life happily and peacefully, without trouble and strife. He wanted to lie in bed at daybreak watching the beams of morning sunlight stream across his queen's lovely face. He wanted to romp in the castle yard with his sons after supper. He wanted to spend his days helping the peasants who came to him in pain and sorrow and need and to enjoy his Sabbaths amid the heavenly echoes of the chapel.

What he did not want to do was to fight a dragon. He had never even seen a dragon, even though he was a king and kings normally see more dragons than the rest of us. Besides, he told himself, he was not a mighty warrior like his father. He was a man of peace, not a man of violence. He was a man of love, not a man of war. He would rather give up his crown than fight a dragon. And yet, he reminded himself, my queen has been taken. She may be wounded. I must rescue her. But what can I do against a dragon?

Filled with confusion and gloom, King Abraham walked into the castle garden and fell to his knees. "O Lord," he groaned, "if it is possible, take this from me. Free my beloved and bring her safely home."

As he prayed, King Abraham thought he heard a rumbling voice say in a language that sounded like Latin, "Take up the book and read." Raising his eyes, he saw a small, thick book lying on the garden bench. It belonged to Augustine, the master who tutored Abraham's two sons.

Trembling, he opened the book and his eyes fastened on these words:

"The violence of death can none avoid who is born mortal; so also against the violence of love can the world do nothing, for as death is most violent to take away, so love is most violent to save."

Love is most violent to save. The words hit King Abraham like a club. He said the words over and over in his mind. Love is most violent to save. Tingling with a strange mixture of joy and fear, Abraham stuffed the book into his shirt. Setting his face like flint, he slipped his favorite sword into his belt, mounted his horse, and rode out the castle gate toward the east, his mind still full of the words he had read. Love is most violent to save.

It was already dark when he arrived at the gate of the dragon king's castle. High up in one of the black towers, he could see the light of a flickering fire. Abraham dismounted and crept toward the gate. Suddenly, he felt something tear his face and head. It clawed at the purple robe he was wearing and tried to trip him.

Franticly, Abraham stepped back, drew his sword, and peered at his invisible adversary. As the full moon broke through the clouds, he saw the castle gate was blocked by thorns. He struck at the thorns with his sword, but they were too tough to cut. Yet he knew that if he were going to rescue his queen, he would have to struggle through this wall, this sea of thorns.

Covering his face as best he could, Abraham bent down and pushed through. Several times he slipped and his knees were slashed. His hands and head and face were scratched and bleeding, his royal robe torn to shreds. After what seemed like hours, he crawled through the last of the thorns

108

and found himself in the entranceway, which branched out into the three main hallways of the castle.

He had no sooner stood up and wiped the blood from his eyes than the room was filled with a blaze of fire. Abraham scrambled behind a pillar. When he looked around it, he saw the dragon king walking toward him down the center hallway.

At the sight, Abraham's heart stopped. The dragon king was nearly as long as the hallway. His red scales glistened despite the darkness. Nothing his father had said could have prepared Abraham for his first sight of a real live dragon.

Gathering his courage, Abraham stepped from behind the pillar and raised his sword. "I have come to rescue my queen!" he announced in the bravest voice he could manage under the circumstances.

Now the dragon saw him for the first time. Cocking his head to one side, he looked at Abraham with hatred and mockery in his eyes.

"Hah!" the dragon laughed, as a cloud of smoke poured from his nostrils. "What do you think I am, coming out with that little toothpick? Come a little closer, and I will turn you into food for my pets."

Swallowing hard, King Abraham tried to speak. His voice squeaked. He cleared his throat and started again. "You are stronger than I, it is true," he said in a quavering voice. "But you have only the violence of death, so you can only take away. I have the violence of love. The violence of love is unconquerable. Love is violent to save."

With a roar, the dragon opened his jaws and breathed out a flood of white hot fire. As Abraham leaped behind the pillar, he felt the blazing heat at his back. When he looked down at his sword, he saw that it had melted to nothing.

"What will you do now, King Abraham?" the dragon sneered. "Even your sword is no good to you."

Abraham knew that he had little hope of saving Sarah, much less himself. His tried to think of a way to trick the dragon, but in the terror of the moment he could think of nothing. A knife. Perhaps he had brought a knife. He fumbled at his belt—no knife. Perhaps his spurs would help—but he had left home in such haste that he had forgotten to wear them. He felt something hard at his breast. Reaching into his shirt, he pulled out Augustine's book.

"What good is a book against a dragon?" he murmured fearfully. "I cannot *read* him to death!"

Just at that moment, the bell in the huge tower clock began to chime the midnight hour. Startled by the sound, the dragon king looked behind him. In the same instant, Abraham started to run down a hallway. The dragon was close behind him. Desperate, King Abraham stopped, turned, threw Augustine's book toward the dragon with all his might, and then ran off down the hallway.

Now, Abraham did not know it (though his father would have), but certain species of dragons have one weakness. They have a soft spot directly on top of the head. Everywhere else, their scales are like armor, but they can be killed by the slightest blow to that one spot. The problem is, however, that it is terribly hard to get close enough to a dragon to hit its soft spot.

As you have probably guessed, the dragon king was exactly the right kind of dragon, and Augustine's book hit the dragon in exactly the right spot. The dragon spun around four and a half times, which is customary, breathed a great cloud of stinking black smoke, and fell to the floor. Dead. Dead as a dragon, as the saying goes.

King Abraham stayed hidden for a long time watching to make sure the dragon was dead. When he was certain, he went through the castle to find Sarah. After a long search, he found her in the dungeon cell, with many of the dragon's victims. King Abraham released them all.

When they found their way back to the castle gate, the wall of thorns had vanished. The sun was rising and filling the world with light and warmth. Taking his queen's hand, the king led the released prisoners back over the mountain to the west, back home to his castle. There, he invited them all to stay for a great feast of thanksgiving. This time, Abraham and Sarah truly did live happily ever after.

MORAL

A wise king winnows the wicked,
and drives the threshing wheel over them.
(Prov. 20:26)

112

Chapter XIII

KING JACOB
OF THE GREEN
GARLAND

nce upon a time there was a king named Eric the Red. He was not called "the Red" for the reason you might guess. His hair was black, he had no beard, and his skin was quite fair. Eric was called "the Red" because that was the color his nose turned when he got drunk from too much wine. And he got drunk a lot.

Eric was a very rich king. He lived in a castle made of black German marble. He wore Chinese silk clothes and sat on a throne made of Indian ivory. He drank French wine from cups made of African gold. At each meal he ate mountains of Russian caviar and bowls of thick red stew, which may have been another reason he was called "the Red." In any case, Eric became immensely fat.

But the people who lived in Eric's kingdom were very poor. They had little to eat and no wine to drink. Their clothes were no better than rags. Some of them had to live in caves because they could not afford to build houses.

In fact, the people were poor for the same reason that King Eric was rich. You see, he stole from them. Every autumn, Eric sent the nobles throughout the land to collect taxes. The nobles took most of the grain and fruit the people harvested. After they left, the orchards looked as if they had been beaten down by hail and the fields as if they had been devoured by locusts.

One day a serf named Nathan came to Eric to complain to the king. Nathan was so angry that he forgot his manners and did not bow before the king.

"My lord, Lord David," Nathan said loudly, "has taken all of my grain harvest this year. I have nothing left to feed my children. Please make Lord David give back some of my harvest, I beg you."

King Eric the Red frowned. "Do you come to the King's throne without bowing?"

Nathan trembled when he realized what he had done. "Your Highness, I did not mean to dishonor you."

Eric rose from his throne. "Guards! Take this man to the prison, and leave him there without food or water for ten days! Then whip him fifty times in the town square!"

The news about Nathan spread throughout the land. No one dared to complain about any of the nobles again. All the people lived in fear of King Eric, his nobles, and his soldiers.

Now Eric had a younger brother named Jacob. Though he was a prince, Jacob did not live with his brother in the castle, and he did not steal from the people. He lived peacefully as a shepherd, tending his flocks and helping his poor neighbors whenever he could.

The people loved Jacob. Safe in their homes, when they thought no soldiers could hear, many whispered that Jacob would make a better king than Eric. But the soldiers did hear, and when they told Eric, he was enraged. Still, Eric was also frightened that Jacob might try to become king. So he threw Jacob into the deepest, darkest cell in the prison.

One evening King Eric was walking in his garden when he heard the rattle of hoofbeats and the blare of a trumpet. Peering over the garden wall, Eric saw thousands of horsemen thundering toward the west gate of the castle. King William the Black, ruler of a distant kingdom, was coming to claim Eric's throne. Eric's heart melted within him. He had no time to gather his soldiers to fight. He ran to the stables, jumped on his red horse (which may have been yet another reason he was called "the Red"), and rode out the east gate. The horse could not run very fast carrying the fat King Eric. An arrow struck Eric in his belly. Biting his lip, he tried to pull it out, but it was already buried in fat. Leaning on his horse's neck, Eric raced away.

Eric did not stop until it was night. By that time, he was deep in the eastern wilderness and had lost his way. His horse collapsed under him and died. It was raining, and Eric's side was bleeding. He was hungry, cold, and tired. Eric found a patch of grass, and ate it, chewing like a cow. He drank muddy water from a puddle, lapping like a dog. He found a dry place under a tree and went to sleep, nestled in the leaves like a bear. The rain stopped during the night, but by morning Eric was covered with dew.

Eric the Red ate grass and drank muddy water in the eastern wilderness for many days. His hair began to look like the wings of a great bird, and his fingernails grew into claws. The wound in his belly became worse. He shivered with cold and burned with fever all at the same time. Eric the Red was dying.

115

He was startled from sleep one morning by a stinging pain in his side. When Eric opened his eyes, Jacob was leaning over him, pouring wine into his wound. Some of Jacob's friends stood nearby, watching in silence. When he saw that Eric was awake, Jacob offered him a drink of cool, clean water.

"How have you come here?" Eric asked after he drank some water.

"When King William invaded the land, he released all of your prisoners. He did not know I was a prince, so he freed me with the rest. My companions and I fled to the wilderness for fear he would try to kill me if he found out who I was."

Eric cried out as Jacob poured more wine into his wound. "Do not waste your wine on me. I am dying. Before I die, I must appoint an heir to take my throne."

Eric's eyes filled with tears. His voice was a raspy whisper. "I was an evil king. I was neither kind nor just, and I have fallen, as I deserved. You must swear to me that if you should ever take my throne, you will not do as I have done."

"With all my heart, I swear it," said Jacob.

Eric tried to speak the way he had once spoken from his ivory throne. "I, King Eric the Red, rightful King of this realm do solemnly and in the sight of God declare that you, Prince Jacob, are king in my place. May you rule all this realm, from the sea to the river, and from the mountains to the plain."

In great pain, Eric turned over. "With what shall I crown you? I must give you a crown," he said. Eric tore some branches from a nearby bush and with shaking hands wound them into a garland. He was barely breathing. "Here is your crown. I crown you King Jacob of the Green Garland."

When he had finished speaking, King Eric the Red died.

116

Jacob's companions looked at one another. Then all together they shouted in a loud voice, "The king is dead! Long live the king!"

Months passed, then years. The people of Eric's kingdom learned that William was no better than Eric had been. William had brought his own soldiers and friends who stole food and money from the people and made themselves rich and fat. Even Eric's nobles hated William.

When the nobles learned that Jacob had escaped, they fled into the wilderness to find him. Jacob soon had an army large and strong enough to take the throne from William.

One overcast day, Jacob made a surprise attack on the east gate of the castle. The battle lasted for two days. By the morning of the third day, the victory was his and Jacob sat on the great ivory throne and walked in the garden.

The first thing Jacob did was to free all those William had sent to prison. He gave Eric's son, who had become lame, a room in his castle and a seat at the king's table.

The next Christmas, Jacob was eating dinner with Bishop Henry when one of the servants came in.

"Begging your pardon, Your Highness. But there is a crowd of peasants gathering outside. They say the winter has been so harsh that they have no food."

Jacob looked at Henry. "What do you think, Bishop Henry?"

Bishop Henry scratched his bald head. "I believe ve must do somesing to satisfy zem. Othervise, zey may become dangerous. I have seen zese peasants ven zey are angry. It is not pretty sight."

"What do you propose?"

"Since you asked, I vill give you my advice. Ve must first make sure zey do not become violent. Zat above all ve must do. And ve must not appear veak or too generous. Zat ve must avoid at all costs. I suggest zat you send a loaf of bread for each family. Zat vill fill their bellies. Zey vill go home and fall asleep. Tomorrow, perhaps zey vill not be angry anymore. If zey return, ve will resort to stern measures."

Jacob stared at the table full of food. He picked up a golden cup and a smile crossed his face.

"Vat are you thinking?" Henry recognized that smile, and he did not like it.

"I will do as you have advised. But I will also do more. I will give a cup of wine and a loaf of bread to each family. And I will let each of them keep a golden cup for himself."

"I do not think zat is a good idea," Henry said, frowning. "Zey vill come to expect it. If you give zem gold now, vat vill zey vant next time? And, besides, zey vant you to live like a king."

"My dear Bishop Henry," said King Jacob. "I think you are wrong about the good people of this land. Once the winter snows have melted, they will be in their fields, plowing and planting. As for living like a king, my brother did quite enough of that."

When Jacob appeared in the castle courtyard, the peasants cheered and clapped their frozen hands. He gave a loaf of bread and a cup of wine to each. They shouted, "Long live King Jacob!"

The next spring, Jacob decided to travel throughout his land to meet his subjects. Bishop Henry did not think it was a good idea, so Jacob did it anyway.

At every town, Jacob sat under a tree wearing his green garland. He listened as the people brought their complaints, and he passed judgments. At one town, Lord David came to the king. He was followed by his serf, Nathan.

118

"Your Highness." Lord David bowed lower than usual.

"Lord David. Have you a complaint to bring before the king?"

"Your Highness, Most Great and Most Just King. You are like the radiance of the sun. This man, Nathan, is a very poor worker. He has been found sleeping three times this week when he should have been working. He works so slowly, Sire, that his work is never finished. Because of this, I have suffered great loss. He tells me he cannot pay what he owes me. Knowing that you are like an angel, knowing good and evil, I beg you, O King, to make Nathan pay fully." Lord David again bowed very low.

King Jacob motioned to Nathan. "Stand before me."

Frightened, Nathan stood in front of the king, his eyes lowered to the ground.

"Is it true what Lord David says about you?"

Nathan said nothing.

"Answer me. Is it true?"

Nathan looked sideways at Lord David, but said nothing.

"Nathan. If you do not answer me, I shall hold you in contempt of my majesty, and you shall be thrown into prison. Why do you sleep when you should be working? Do you not have the Sabbath day to rest?"

Nathan looked straight at King Jacob. "No, Your Highness. I do not."

"What? You mean Lord David forces you to work seven days a week!"

Nathan nodded. "Yes, Sire."

"Lord David," Jacob said sternly. "You know the laws of this land. You know that every servant or peasant, no matter how low, is to have the Sabbath day to rest from his work. As punishment, you must pay back twice what you have taken from Nathan in the past. And as for you," Jacob turned to Nathan, "You are from this day forward a free man."

Throughout the land, all the people praised King Jacob. They had food to eat, clothes to wear, and houses to live in. They did not fear the king's soldiers or the greedy nobles. Even the weather seemed better: just enough rain in the spring, and just enough sun in the summer.

Meanwhile, King William the Black had returned home to let his soldiers heal their wounds. He was angry and swore that he would someday take back the kingdom from Jacob.

Before breakfast one morning, King Jacob was walking in his garden when he heard the rattle of hoofbeats and the blare of a trumpet. Peering over the garden wall, Jacob saw thousands of horsemen thundering across the plain toward the west gate of the castle. It was King William, coming with his army to take the throne again. Jacob's heart melted within him. Most of his soldiers were in the far north fighting the army of King Dagbert, so he was nearly alone and completely unprotected. Jacob ran to the stables, jumped on his white horse, and raced out through the east gate.

There he met an army of peasants carrying tools and clubs, with Nathan in the lead. When Jacob saw them, he turned his horse. Eyes flashing like flames, Jacob led the charge against William's army, swinging his sword and shouting to the peasants to follow.

The battle raged for hours. Soldiers in armor thrust swords and spears at farmers armed with pitchforks and axes. Toward evening, Jacob struck down King William. After that, William's soldiers became confused and began to attack each other. When the sun rose the next morning, not even one of William's soldiers was left to bury the dead.

Jacob's kingdom was never attacked again. He reigned forever after over a peaceful kingdom, and all the world learned of the justice and mercy of King Jacob of the Green Garland.

MORAL

Love and faithfulness keep a king safe;
through love his throne is made secure.
(Prov. 20:28)

Chapter XIV

MERiBAh, the GOATHERD'S BRIDE

nce upon a time, a goatherd who lived on a tall mountain in the north country visited the city south of the river. He brought his flock to the city each year to sell goats, fresh milk, and cheese. Then he would lead whatever goats he had left back to his mountain home in the north.

As he led his goats toward market, he saw a young woman stumble as she pulled a wagon loaded with bricks. She fell to the rocky street, and the wagon tipped over on her leg. As the goatherd ran to help her, she squirmed in a puddle of blood, trying to pull her leg free of the wagon.

The goatherd lifted up the wagon and tore off a piece of his shirt to bandage her leg. Then, for the first time, he looked at her. Her hair was thick as sheep's wool. Though she was not especially beautiful, and in fact rather plain, with one look the goatherd fell deeply in love. He asked her name.

"Meribah," she replied, smiling in a way that made her face look sad. "Ow! Don't press so hard. I thought you were trying to help!"

"Sorry." The goatherd wiped away the blood. "There, that should be clean now. Not too much damage."

Meribah's face twisted in pain. "Do you think I will ever walk again? It hurts so much!"

"Oh, I think you will walk again," the goatherd answered as he helped Meribah to her feet. He looked at the ground for an awkward moment, trying to think of something to say. "Do you live here in the city?" he finally asked, though he knew she did.

"I am a household slave to the nobleman who lives there," she said, pointing to a large house at the end of the street.

"That must be a very comfortable place to work," the goatherd said as they began walking toward the house, with the goatherd pulling the wagon of bricks.

"Ach!" she said. "It is awful. I have to work day and night. I get little sleep and not even a day off. He makes me move bricks from one end of the world to another. And the food they feed us—Ach! It is terrible. Here we are." Meribah smiled again, and her face looked even sadder.

As she limped down the pathway toward the house, the goatherd called after her, "I hope to see you again."

The goatherd could not forget Meribah's sadness, which made him feel the way he did when he watched a cold rain outside a window on a dark afternoon. He tried to think of some way to save her from her terrible slavery. Rummaging through his pockets, he found a few coins, but not nearly enough to redeem her. He knew he could not sell enough goat's milk cheese to pay for her. What else? He counted up his goats.

"If I sold twenty," he thought, "perhaps I would have money to buy her. That would leave me with twelve goats to start another flock. And I would have a little extra to buy Meribah a linen dress."

That evening, the goatherd appeared at the door of the house Meribah had shown him. A butler led him to the nobleman's chambers, where he was just sitting down to his dinner.

"I would like to redeem your slave Meribah."

The nobleman looked at the goatherd's shabby clothes. "Can you afford her?"

"Oh, yes," the goatherd said. "I have sold twenty goats." He stretched out his hand to show his money.

"Fifteen pieces of silver? It usually takes thirty," the nobleman replied. "But, in Meribah's case, perhaps I can make an exception. You may have her."

The goatherd nearly threw the money into the air. He wanted to dance and shout and hug the nobleman. But he only smiled. "What do you plan to do with her?" the nobleman asked.

"I love her," the goatherd answered. "I plan to marry her."

The nobleman looked at him with surprise and pity. "Well, then. She may leave immediately. Get out by midnight. That is when we close the gates."

The goatherd rushed to Meribah's room to tell her the news. She did not seem very happy, but she let the goatherd help her pack her belongings. As the clock in the city square was striking twelve, they walked through the gates of the great house into the city street.

The next day, they were married in a chapel of the city cathedral, with Meribah wearing her new white linen dress. "We should set out immediately," the goatherd said after the wedding. "It will take forty days to get to our home on the mountain."

With the goatherd leading the way and Meribah and the twelve remaining goats following, they set out toward the river. At first, Meribah was happy to be free. But the more she listened to her husband, the more she realized he lived in a very small house, had only twelve goats, and could offer few comforts to a wife. Even before they crossed the river, she had begun to regret leaving the nobleman's house.

"You do not expect me to get my clothes wet, do you?" she asked when they got to the river.

The goatherd thought a moment. "Let's do this. You climb on my back. I will spread out my arms, like this—like wings—and carry you across." Meribah did not much like the idea, but she let him carry her across the river. She screamed the whole way and twice nearly made her husband fall over. When he finally got her across the river, he went back and carried each of his twelve goats to the other side.

They had been traveling for three days when the land became very dry. All the streams had dried up, and there were no wells in sight. Because the goats had no water, they stopped giving milk. One morning, the goatherd climbed a mountain hoping to find some sign of water. As he turned the corner of the narrow trail, he saw an astonishing sight. A stream of water was flowing out of the mountain, from a spring buried deep in the rock. The goatherd gathered every container he could, filled them with water, and hurried back to camp to tell Meribah of his discovery.

"Look!" he cried. "Water! I've got water!"

"Where did it come from?" she asked.

"I was climbing on the mountain and there it was, coming from inside the mountain! It was amazing!"

"What do you plan to do with that water?" Meribah asked.

"Drink it, of course. It is our life. If we do not have water, we will die!"

"You expect me to drink water that came out of a mountain?" Meribah asked sharply. "It is probably dirty. Who knows what kind of animals have done who knows what in that water? Oh, no, sir. I will not drink water from a rock. At least," she added wistfully, "at least we always had plenty of water at the nobleman's house. Oh, I wish I had stayed. It was so pleasant and comfortable there!"

The goatherd pleaded with her. She finally agreed to drink, but the water tasted so bitter to her that she drank only a few drops. Day after day, she drank a few drops, complaining with each swallow. Eventually, the goatherd became so tired of her complaints that he moved out of the tent and slept outside.

Finally it rained, and the streams filled with water. The goatherd and his bride would not be thirsty again.

One night during the next week, an animal came into their camp and ate all their food. When they awoke in the morning, there was nothing to eat. As far as the eye could see, there was no town or even a farm where they might find bread.

"We are going to starve, aren't we?" Meribah said. "Is this why you brought me out here? To starve me to death? Oh, it was better in the nobleman's house. I may have been a slave, but at least we had bread."

The goatherd became so tired of her complaints that he moved out of the camp altogether, and slept among his goats.

A few days later, he noticed a small kid wandering up a mountain. Leaving the others, he followed the kid. Before he

knew it, he was so high he seemed to have entered heaven. Clouds swirled around him, but the kid was nowhere to be seen.

Then the goatherd saw an astonishing thing. A field of golden wheat was growing on top of one of the clouds, as ripe and thick as could be. If only I could get some, he thought. Then we could make bread.

Just then, the wind changed and the cloud moved toward him, stopping right next to him. Not quite knowing what he was doing, the goatherd carefully put a foot onto the cloud. He sank a bit into the softness, but then his foot stopped. He grasped the cloud with his fingers and pulled himself up. With shaking knees, he stood up and found himself balancing on top of a cloud.

He carefully made his way to the wheat and gathered as much as he could carry, before leaping back onto the mountain. As quickly as it had appeared, the cloud was blown away.

The goatherd ran down the mountain calling out to Meribah.

"Why are you making such a noise again?" she demanded. "I was trying to get a few hours of rest before I starve to death."

"Sorry, dear," the goatherd said quietly. "But I could not help it. Something amazing has happened. I was following a kid up the mountain and I came across a wheat field on a cloud. Look at all the wheat I gathered. It is enough to feed us for many days."

"Did you find the kid?" Meribah asked.

"Yes, dear. I found it on the way down. But, look, we will not starve."

129

"You want me to eat bread from a cloud? How do I know what it really is? Oh, no, sir, you will not get me to eat bread from the sky. Besides, I am in the mood for meat. I was tired of bread anyway. Since you caught that kid, why don't we eat him for supper?"

The goatherd pleaded, and Meribah finally agreed to eat bread made from the wheat of the sky. Still she complained that she had no meat.

"But there is no meat, dear," the goatherd told her again and again.

"There is. Why don't you kill those miserable goats of yours? We could eat them."

"But then we would have no milk, butter, or cheese, and nothing to sell in the village when we get back to our home on the mountain," the goatherd explained. "With these twelve goats, I will begin a new flock, which will become as numerous as the stars in the sky."

"Oh, you are dreaming. Don't make excuses. Get me some meat."

Soon after this, as the goatherd led the goats to a grassy pasture, he saw another astonishing sight. Spread out before him on a hillside were hundreds and hundreds of fat quail. Instead of flying away when he came near, they sat still. The goatherd plucked up one bird after another, tied their feet together, and hurried back to tell Meribah. Now she will be happy, he thought. We have meat.

"Look at what I found. I was leading the goats on the mountain, and I came across hundred and hundreds of birds. It was as if they wanted me to catch them. Now, we shall have meat enough for our whole journey."

"Ach!" Meribah answered. "I really was hoping for some red meat. But I suppose this is better than nothing."

130

The goatherd slaughtered and dressed two fat quail hens for dinner and cooked them over the open fire. He set one down steaming in front of Meribah.

"This looks delicious," he said.

"I guess it will do," Meribah answered. "It is not nearly so good as the meat we had back in the city."

They ate in silence for a while, with the goatherd relishing each bite, and Meribah picking at her food and making faces, just the way you do when your mother serves liver or broccoli.

"By the way," she said suddenly, her mouth full of food. "I have been wanting to talk with you about your little hut on the mountain. I think it will be much too small. Maybe we should move into the village. I do not think I can stand living on the mountain."

"But the mountain is my home. I want you to live with me as my wife on my land. It really is a good land," the goatherd answered. "Besides, if we moved to the village, I would not be able to tend my goats."

"Ach! The land does not sound so good to me. That reminds me of another thing," she said, her mouth still full of quail. "Why don't you get rid of those goats? No one likes goat's milk cheese anyway. I know I don't. Why not get some sheep?"

"I tried sheep once," the goatherd replied. "They are hard to handle. They are so stubborn. If they do not get their way, they put up such a fuss. I would rather be a goatherd."

That night, while the goatherd slept among his goats, it began to rain. He crawled under a tree and listened to the rain pounding on the roof of Meribah's tent. He was just drifting to sleep when a sound louder than rain on a tin roof made him sit up. It was coming from the tent. He jumped up

131

and ran to the tent to find Meribah coughing and sputtering, her face looking white as wool.

"The quail," she whispered in a hoarse voice. "It was poison!" The rain pounded so loudly on the tent roof that the goatherd could hardly hear her speak.

"But I'm not sick," the goatherd cried.

"It was poison, I tell you. Oh, I should never have left the nobleman's house. I have come all this way to die in the wilderness. Why did I ever listen to you? Why did I ever agree to marry you? I should never have left the city! If I live through the night, I am going back first thing next morning." When she had spoken these words, Meribah gasped and became silent. At the same moment, the rain stopped.

It is a horrible thing to record, but, as it turned out, that was Meribah's last breath. Her husband sat by her bed all night, hoping she would revive, but she did not. In the morning, he buried her body in the wildernss, then continued his journey back to his mountain home.

The goatherd lived for many more years, tending his goats and traveling every year to the city south of the river. But he never remarried, and he never bought any sheep.

MORAL

It is better to live in a desert land,
than with a contentious and vexing woman.
(Prov. 21:19)

Chapter XV

A Cloud of Birds

here was once a farmer who was very poor. He had a few animals: five or six skinny chickens that laid tiny yellow eggs, a dirty old goat, and a scrawny cow that gave thin, watery milk. He had a small piece of land, but for many years the ground was too dry and hard to grow anything. The wind blew across the fields, stirring up huge dust clouds, so that the land looked like a smoking furnace. His little red barn had turned grey from neglect, and it looked as if you could blow it down if you had a mind to do that sort of thing.

The farmer tried everything to make his little farm prosper. He went to meetings to learn about the most scientific methods of farming. He borrowed money to buy the newest fertilizers and the most powerful machinery. He bought the best seed and special mineral water to make it grow. Nothing worked. His wife told him over and over he should sell the farm and look for a better way to make a living.

One winter morning, the farmer found his chickens frozen in the yard. In the barn, the goat was dead. The farmer was left with his scrawny cow and his dry, dusty land. It was then that he made up his mind to listen to his wife, sell his farm and his cow, and seek to make his living away from the farm. He tied a rope around the cow's neck and set off to the butcher's shop. His wife watched him from the porch of the house as he disappeared down the road.

Before long, she looked out a window to see her husband returning from town, still leading the cow. Puzzled, she ran to meet him and asked if something was wrong.

For a few moments the farmer stared at the ground and said nothing. "On my way to town," the farmer said slowly, "I met a bearded man dressed in a hairy robe lying on his side beside the road, looking off into the distance. His face looked as if it were carved from stone. I wanted to walk by without even looking at him, but I stopped. Then this man fixed a glittering eye on me, and . . ."

"A what?" his wife interrupted.

"You know. A glittering eye. Like this." The farmer curled his brow and squinted with what he hoped was a penetrating look in his eyes.

His wife only laughed. "Oh, go on."

"Well, I will tell you. He stared so long and so hard that I wanted to move on, but I was planted to the spot. Then he asked me where I was going with the cow. I told him I was going to sell her to the butcher in town, and I explained all the animals were dead, and nothing would grow, and our land was turning into a desert, and . . ."

The farmer shivered, remembering how frightened he was as the man talked with him.

"Well, what happened then?" his wife asked impatiently.

"He reached into his robe, and pulled out a small bag and handed it to me." The farmer stopped again.

"What was in it? What was in the bag? Money? Did you sell him the farm?"

Reluctantly, the farmer pulled the bag from his shirt and opened it to show his wife.

"Birdseed!" she cried. "What do we need birdseed for? Our chickens died last night!"

"That is what I told him," the farmer said. He was beginning to lose patience too. "But the man told me if I spread out a few seeds inside the barn every morning and evening, birds would come. Birds, and much more. That is what he said, 'Birds, and much more.' Then he turned over on his other side with his back to me and stared off into the distance."

His wife gave her husband a disgusted look. "Why, you do not believe this, do you? Magic seeds? Now, you get to town and sell that cow."

"Well, it may be worth a try," the farmer said quietly. "We do not have anything to lose, do we?" His wife would not look at him. "I cannot describe the feeling I had when he gave me these seeds. I just believe him."

"Well, do what you want," his wife said. "I will just sit here and starve."

The farmer turned toward the barn and said over his shoulder, "He told me something else too. We have to feed the birds in the barn every morning and evening, and we have to make sure the barn stays clean. We have to clean up every morning and evening."

"Do what you want," his wife said with a snort.

As the sun was setting that evening, the farmer climbed up the broken ladder into the loft of the barn, and spread a few seeds on the floor. Then he and his wife went to bed.

They were awakened in the morning by a sound like a marching army, like thunder, like loud trumpets, like a waterfall. So loud was the clamor that it made the bedposts rattle. Leaping from bed, the farmer pushed open the shutters and looked out toward his old grey barn.

The sun was just rising over the barn roof. The sky was filled with honking, screaming, singing birds of every color and size. It seemed the sun itself had turned gold, blue, and scarlet and had sprouted wings. The birds darted back and forth, moving as if tied together by invisible string. When the sun's rays flashed among the birds, they looked like a cloud of fire.

The farmer and his wife laughed like children. They loved the sound and sight of birds, and they knew the birdseed had drawn the birds to the barn. The farmer knew somehow that his life would be happier now. Something told him that his land was not doomed after all.

That night, a dark thundering cloud appeared on the horizon and brought such a soaking rain as the farmer had not seen in years. When the rain ended, the farmer planted his few remaining seeds. Within days, there were sprouts everywhere. A dozen wheat stalks appeared for every seed he planted. Before summer, his garden was full of carrots, potatoes, pumpkins, tomatoes, heads of lettuce and cabbage, and beans. Trees he had forgotten bowed low under the weight of their luscious fruit.

He had more than enough to feed himself and his wife and sold what they did not eat in the town market. He bought some chickens, who laid eggs so large that each could feed a family of five for three days. The cow grew fat and gave pure cream.

The farmer rebuilt his old barn to make the birds more comfortable. And every morning and evening, even in the coldest days of winter, the farmer dutifully climbed the ladder to the barn loft to clean up after the birds and to give them more seeds to eat. When he was sick, his wife bundled

136

herself in a blanket and climbed up to feed the birds. Some-how, the bag of birdseed was never empty, and the thou-sands of birds were filled and satisfied with the few seeds he fed them each day.

The next year was even better. They made so much money selling vegetables, milk, and eggs that they were able to buy more land. The year after that, the farmer tore down his little cottage and built a mansion of white marble that gleamed like a diamond. He bought even more land, and all his farms continued to flourish.

The farmer himself grew fat and became fond of expen-sive clothes. He wore robes woven of gold, blue, purple, and scarlet thread. The tailor made him shirts with a dozen jewels sewn in rows across the breast and golden chains hung from the shoulders.

The farmer and his wife prospered for as many years as they had been poor. They hired men to work the land, and women to cook meals and clean house. The farmer became the richest man in the land, and there was talk of his becom-ing governor. He began to think that things had never been any different.

For many years, the farmer remembered every morning and evening to feed the birds in the loft of his barn and to clean up their home. Then, on one especially cold winter morning, he and his wife decided to stay under their thick quilts. That evening, they forgot about the birds, and the next morning was too cold again.

At first, they made up excuses. The ladder was unsafe for so fat a man as the farmer, and his wife was not as young as she used to be. The farmer felt silly asking one of his hired men to feed songbirds. Besides, the farmer thought, how could feeding a flock of birds have helped his farm? Eventu-

ally, the farmer convinced himself his prosperity was a product of his own wisdom and skill, and he forgot about the birds altogether.

For several days, and then for several weeks, and then for several months, neither the farmer nor his wife ever climbed the ladder; they never fed the birds and never cleaned the barn. Most of the birds stayed around the farm, but some began to search elsewhere for food. The barn became filthy, "an abomination," one of the hired men called it.

The next spring, there was less rain than usual. The sky turned gray and hard like iron. The chickens laid fewer and smaller eggs. The cow began to lose weight, and her milk became thinner and thinner. The land became dry and hard as bronze. For several years, there was little rain, and even when there was rain, nothing grew.

The farmer again tried everything to make his farm prosper. He bought the best seeds and the best food for his animals, used the best fertilizers, and tried all the newest and most scientific farming methods. Nothing worked.

Because he could no longer afford to pay them, the farmer let his field men and household servants go. To pay his debts, he began to sell land. His gleaming marble house became dirty and broken down. After a few years, the farm was as dead as it had been before. The farmer had only his expensive robes to show that he had ever been rich, and they looked out of place on such a poor farm.

Late one evening, there was a knock at the farmer's door. When the farmer opened it, there stood the bearded man in the hairy robes who had given him the birdseed so many years before. He walked past the farmer and took a seat by the hearth. Then he fixed a glittering eye on the farmer. "So that is a glittering eye," his wife thought to herself, shivering.

"I told you to feed the birds in your barn, and keep it clean," the man said. "Every morning and evening. I told you."

The farmer had not thought of the birds in years.

"Why do you think that your farm has died?"

"I do not know. Perhaps I have been using the wrong kind of seed. Perhaps I have not been watering enough, or watering too much. I have heard about a new fertilizer. . . ."

"You should have followed my instructions," the bearded man interrupted. "If you want your farm to prosper, you need to clean up the barn. You must begin to feed the birds again. Every morning and evening. Otherwise, all the birds will leave forever and your farm will die."

The farmer looked at the man in silence for a moment, before bursting into scornful laughter. "When I first met you, I believed what you said. I believed that feeding those birds could help me. Can you imagine? I really did believe it! My wife told me it was all foolishness. But I was ready to try anything. But what have those birds to do with my farm? Nothing! Absolutely nothing! Farming is a science. It is not magic. You are full of fairy tales and superstitions. Now, get out of my house."

The bearded man did not move. "I told you to get out," the farmer snarled, reaching to take the man by the collar. The bearded man pushed him away, and as he did, he tore the golden chain from the shoulder of the farmer's beautiful robe. "Look at what you have done!" the farmer screamed. "Now get out!"

As the man stepped into the night, he fixed his glittering eye on the farmer. "I warn you. Do as I say, or your land will die forever!" The farmer slammed the door in his face.

140

Early the next morning, the farmer and his wife awoke to a sound like thunder, like a marching army, like a trumpet, like a waterfall. They dashed to the window and threw open the shutters. Outside, a sunlit cloud of birds hovered over the roof of the barn. As they watched, the cloud darted this way and that, and then, with a great thunder of wings and song, flew off toward the east until it disappeared. And the farmer never saw the birds again.

MORAL

*When you set your eyes on (wealth),
it is gone. For wealth certainly makes itself
wings, like an eagle that flies
toward the heavens.*
(Prov. 23:5)

141

Chapter XVI

Che Labors
of Braxcon hicks

nce there was a young man named Braxton Hicks. Now, I know as well as anyone that characters in fairy tales are not supposed to have last names. Just this once, it is important. If you don't believe me, go ask your mother.

Anyway, Braxton Hicks was not your typical hero. He never went on any adventures. His mother never tried to lose him in the forest (though the thought did cross her mind from time to time), and the few dwarves in his town did not even know any card tricks, much less magic spells. Braxton liked to stay home. He rarely left his room; to be perfectly honest, he rarely got out of bed.

Of course, Braxton kept very busy. He had a lot to do and a lot to worry about. He had to go to the kitchen three or eight times a day to find food. Some days, there was very little in the cupboard the first few times, so he would have to go ten or thirteen times. Sometimes, he had to yell at his old mother before she would fix enough food for him. Yelling at your mother is extremely hard work. And Braxton had to turn over in bed every now and then, which was not as easy for Braxton Hicks as it is for you or me.

Besides that, Braxton Hicks had a special gift. He was able to see things ordinary people did not see and to understand things ordinary people could never understand. Because he had so much time to think, he could think about everything in the world. He was full of ideas about how to make the world a better place. He felt deep within that he must be a child of the gods. He was quite certain that he had been given special wisdom to set the world right.

You might be wondering how Braxton Hicks could set the world right if he never left his bed. How could he share his special wisdom if he never talked with anyone? Braxton himself wondered about that very same thing. He lay on his bed worrying and wondering for years and years, but he could not think of an answer.

One day, Braxton's old mother died. At first, Braxton was sad, but after a few days, he concluded it was for the best. "Now that I no longer have to care for my mother," he thought, "I will be able to go into the world. I will finally have a chance to set the world right by sharing my special wisdom with everyone I meet."

The very next day Braxton put the last few scraps of food into a pack and set off. He had gone only a short way when he saw a man weeding a garden. The man looked very tired, and sweat was streaming down his brow.

"Good morning!" Braxton shouted. The man looked up but said nothing. Braxton watched him for a moment, then said as politely as he could, "Excuse me. You are doing that all wrong. There is a much better way to do that."

The man glared at him. "You know how to weed a garden, do you?"

Braxton smiled. "I have always wanted a garden of my very own. Will you let me work a while?"

The gardener thought for a moment, looked back and forth, shrugged his shoulders, and said, "I suppose you could work while I get something to drink. But listen. You need to pull these thistles here. And there has been a boar crashing through the fence and trampling the turnips. If you see him coming, try to catch him or at least stop him."

Braxton nodded eagerly. "I will take care of things. Do not worry about your garden. I will guard it with my life."

The man stood slowly and walked off stiffly toward the town tavern. He called over his shoulder, "Don't tell anyone I let you do this. The owner of the garden is on a long journey, but I do not want him to know that I am taking time off."

Braxton Hicks knelt down along the first row of turnips. He cut his finger on the spiny stem of the first weed. After carefully pulling up three or four weeds, Braxton realized it was getting very hot. Then, he felt sweat dripping down his back. "Time for a short rest," he thought. Finding a shady spot under a tree, Braxton lay down and fell asleep.

He slept only a moment, or so it seemed, before he was awakened by a terrifying noise. A boar had crashed through the fence, splintering wood in every direction. Most of the vegetables were already crushed or eaten, and the carefully plowed garden had been churned into a muddy mess. At the far end of the garden, Braxton saw the grunting boar rooting for the last few turnips.

Remembering the gardener's instructions, Braxton crept up behind the boar, leaped on its back, and grabbed its ears. This is not the best way to introduce oneself to a raging boar. The startled animal squealed and bolted through the hole in the fence, dragging a surprised Braxton Hicks along

145

behind. The boar ran through a field, and down the main street of town, squealing as he went. As they neared the town tavern, the gardener was coming out after having a few too many glasses of beer. He stared and rubbed his eyes.

"What have you done to my garden?" he bellowed.

Barely able to breathe, Braxton shouted back, "Don't worry! I will come back and fix everything!"

"Oh, no, you will not!" Braxton heard the gardener say as the boar dragged him out the other end of town. "If you try to come back to my garden, I will kill you! I will kill you!"

It was late afternoon before Braxton Hicks finally had the idea of letting go of the boar's ears. By then, the boar had dragged him far to the east of town. There was only one small house in sight, high up on a hill. With shaking legs, Braxton climbed the hill and knocked at the door.

A young man answered. He was Braxton's own age and size. In fact, he looked so much like Braxton that they could have been brothers.

"Please, can you give me some food and water?" Braxton hissed through his dried lips. "I am far from my home and have no way back."

"I do not give to beggars," the young man said, as he began to close the door.

"I am no beggar. How could you think such a thing? My, my, do I look like a beggar? No matter. I will work in your fields if you wish. Anything you ask. Just give me some food and water, please."

The young farmer thought a moment, and then opened the door. "All right. Tomorrow I have some harvesting to do, and I could use another pair of hands."

The next morning, he took Braxton to the fields and showed him the tall hay he was to cut and bundle. "I have

146

thought a lot about farming," Braxton said cheerfully as he swung the scythe this way and that. "I am sure that there is a better way to cut hay. When I am finished, farming will never be the same."

After watching Braxton for a few minutes, the young man left to work in another part of the field. Braxton had swung the scythe a few more times when he realized how hot it was. His hands were beginning to blister. A few swings later, he felt sweat trickling down his back. "Time for a short rest," he thought. There were no trees, so Braxton lay down in the middle of the hay and fell asleep.

As he slept, Braxton dreamed he was using his scythe to fight a nine-headed monster. Every time he cut off a head, two new ones grew back in its place. He swung furiously back and forth, but he could not kill the monster.

Braxton opened his eyes to see a face peering at him. His mind still full of his strange dream, Braxton rose up in the field and struck at the face with his scythe, nearly cutting off the head of the young farmer who could have been his brother.

"What are you doing?" the young man cried, pointing at the spots of blood on the ground. "You hit me in the cheek with that thing. You nearly killed me!"

"I thought you were a nine-headed monster," Braxton answered lamely.

"Why aren't you working?" the young man asked. When Braxton did not answer, the farmer said, "I think I made a mistake. You had better leave. And do not ever come back."

Tired and hungry, Braxton returned to the highway and wandered off toward the east. When he reached the top of the next hill, he saw the sea stretch out before him like glass. Huddled against the shore was a small village. A ship was anchored in the shallow waters, its mast tall as an oak.

147

"I have always wanted to be a sailor," Braxton thought to himself. "I am sure I would be a very great sailor. And if I travel from place to place, I will be able to share my special wisdom with everyone. I will truly be able to set the world right. No one in my own land appreciates my great wisdom anyway. All great geniuses are misunderstood. It is time to take my wisdom to the wider world."

Braxton Hicks found the ship's captain and asked for work. Several sailors were ill, so the captain readily agreed to hire him.

"What is your cargo?" Braxton asked.

"Golden apples," the captain replied. "And when we get to the next port, we will pick up ivory, baboons, and other animals."

The next morning, the ship drew up its anchor and set off. At first, Braxton felt sick as the ship rolled back and forth, but he soon got used to it. When they had been sailing for three hours, he reported to the captain.

"What would you like me to do, sir?"

"Go below into the cargo hold. You will find crates full of golden apples. Make sure that none are broken and none of the apples are damaged. Stack the crates, count them, and report back to me."

Below deck, Braxton picked up a crate and got a splinter in his finger. He picked up another and realized how hot and stuffy it was in the hold of the ship. When he picked up the third, he felt a river of sweat flowing down his back. "Time for a short rest," he thought, and he lay down on top of the crates of apples and fell into a deep sleep.

While Braxton Hicks was sleeping, dark clouds formed in the sky. Thunder boomed and lightning crackled through the salty air. Rain came, as if the windows of heaven were opened. The sea tossed and churned, as if the fountains of the deep were broken up. Still Braxton Hicks slept.

When lightning struck the main mast, it split the deck with the force of its fall. The sailors and even the captain scrambled into lifeboats and desperately rowed away from the doomed ship. Still Braxton Hicks slept.

I would like to tell you that Braxton Hicks awoke, rebuked the wind and the waves, and was saved. I would like to tell you that a great fish swallowed Braxton Hicks and carried him to safety. I would like to tell you that he was marooned on a desert island and taught the natives the ways of civilized men. But things like that are too strange for fairy tales. They only happen in real life.

In fact, Braxton Hicks never woke up. He slept as the water filled the hold of the ship. He slept as the ship sank. As the thunder crashed outside, he lay peacefully snoring on top of the crates of golden apples. And I suppose he is still sleeping there to this day.

MORAL

As the door turns on its hinges,
so does the sluggard on his bed. The sluggard
buries his hand in the dish; he is weary of
bringing it to his mouth again.
The sluggard is wiser in his own eyes,
than seven men who can give a discreet answer.
(Proverbs 26:14-16)

149

Chapter XVII

The King
From the Tower

There was once a king who lived in a tall tower in the midst of a city. The top of the tower poked through the clouds, so that from his porch, the king could nearly touch the sun, and, though he had never tried it, he was sure that with a little effort he could step onto the moon. He knew he was the highest king in the world.

This king spent his days walking around the porch of his tower, watching the sun rise over the clouds and looking at the curious tiny specks that swarmed through the streets of the city below. Though he was king, he had never visited the city. From what he could see, the only people who lived there were small as ants.

One morning, as he was watching the sunrise, the king decided to visit his subjects. He carefully dressed himself in his most impressive purple robe, buckled the clasp of his golden belt, and put on his shiniest black shoes. He looked at himself in the mirror to make sure he looked like a king. He looked and looked for quite some time. When he was satisfied, he descended the long staircase that led from the tower to the city.

When he reached the bottom of the staircase, he took a deep breath. The tiny people of the city, he thought, would be awestruck at so gigantic a king. Everyone would bow to the ground before him, kiss his feet, and fight for a chance to touch the hem of his robe. He must make every effort to put them at ease. Spreading his hands in a sign of blessing, he stepped out onto the walkway beside the street.

The king noticed immediately that the tiny people of the city were not so tiny as he had thought. Most of them, in fact, were quite a bit larger than the king himself.

He also noticed immediately that no one bowed to him or kissed his feet. Instead, everyone ignored him. The men and women on the walkway hurried past without even looking. One man, reading a book as he walked, slammed into the king, nearly knocking him to the ground, and then walked off without so much as an "Excuse me." Just when the king had regained his balance, a cart rolled by and scattered dust onto his gorgeous purple robe.

It was then that the king noticed that everything in the city looked dry as a desert. There were no fountains in the town square, no puddles on the street, and everyone seemed hot and thirsty.

"I say," he said to the next man who passed by, "I am the king from the high tower. Shouldn't you be bowing or something? Do you want to touch my beautiful purple robe or kiss my shiny black shoes?" But the man only looked suspiciously at the dusty king and crossed to the other side of the street.

For a moment, the king thought he would return to his tower and never come back. It was already clear that no one in the city appreciated or honored him as he deserved. Just then, he spied a wine shop down the street. Being thirsty from his long walk down the staircase, he swaggered up the street and into the wine shop.

"I say," the king said, "give me a bottle of your best wine."

The shopkeeper looked at him and began to laugh. "Give? Give you a bottle of my best wine? We do not give anything away in this shop, buster. Besides, it has been so dry here that water and wine are as valuable as gold."

The king put his nose in the air and sniffed. "But I am different. I am not 'Buster.' I am the king!" he said in a very kingly voice.

"I don't care if you are Julius Caesar," the shopkeeper laughed. "You do not get free wine. And if you are not going to buy anything, get out." The shopkeeper picked up a barrel and threatened to throw it at the king.

Afraid for his life, the king fled from the wine shop. He slowed as he turned down another street and presently he came to a bakery. In the window was the most beautiful wedding cake he had ever seen, and he realized suddenly how hungry one becomes when threatened with a wine barrel. So he strutted into the bakery and up to the counter.

"I say," he said in a most impressive manner. "I would like to have that wedding cake in the window."

The baker looked up and wiped his forehead with his hand, leaving a streak of white flour above his eyes that made him look like a head-hunter from a South Pacific island. "You what?"

"I would like you to give me that cake in the window."

The baker laughed. "Give you that cake? It is already sold. I can't give it to you, fella. I could make you another, just like it, if you pay me."

"No," the king answered. "I want that cake, and no other. Perhaps you do not know who I am. I am not 'Fella.' I am the king from the tower. I demand that you give me that cake in the window."

"I don't care if you are Charles the Great," the baker replied. "I do not give away cakes. If you are not going to buy something, get out. Get out!" The baker hurled a huge lump of dough that missed the king's head by a hair's breadth.

Fearing another mound of dough might smother him, the king sprinted from the bakery into the street. Around another corner, he came to a jeweler's shop. In the window was a sparkling golden crown, covered with diamonds, rubies, emeralds, sapphires. It was more beautiful by far that the king's own crown. When he saw it, he suddenly remembered that he had left his own crown at home in his tower. "Perhaps that is why no one recognizes me," he thought. So, he walked into the jeweler's shop and up to the counter.

"I say," the king began, "I would like to have that crown in the window."

The jeweler looked up from his work and fixed a sharp eye on the king. "Listen, guy. Do you know how much it costs?" he asked.

"No," the king answered with a nervous smile. He was still shaking a bit after his narrow escape at the bakery. "But the cost is not important. You see, I am not 'Guy.' I am the king of the tower. That is the most beautiful crown I have ever seen. I need it so everyone will recognize me. I want you to give it to me."

The jeweler looked surprised at first, then his eyes burned with anger. "Give it to you! I don't care if you are Napoleon Bonaparte, I would not give you that crown. It is worth a fortune. And if you are not going to buy something, get out. Get out!" The jeweler brandished a pair of scissors.

Frightened nearly out of his wits, the king raced out the door and down the walkway. He was so angry he wanted to destroy the city and everyone in it. But then he remembered he had no army and would have a hard time getting soldiers so long as no one knew he was king. This thought filled him with sorrow. "Some king I am," he thought. "None of my subjects even recognizes me, and none obeys me."

The king's thoughts were interrupted by a sound. He stopped in the middle of the walkway and listened. It was very faint at first. As he listened, he realized it was the voice of a child, who seemed to be crying for help.

The king looked at the people around him. None of the others seemed to hear the voice. None stopped to listen. They just kept walking busily up and down the dry street.

"Don't you hear anything?" the king cried out. But the people walked on.

For a moment, the king thought he had imagined the voice. Then it came again. "Help!" This time he was certain he heard it.

The king called again to the hot and thirsty people swirling around him. No one even looked. "Why should I do anything?" he asked himself. "I have more important things to do than to help little children. I am the king, after all." He started back toward his tower. Up in the clouds, he would be at peace. Up in his tower, he would be far too high to hear voices crying for help. When he was up in the clouds, these nasty sweaty people would turn back into the tiny little ants they were supposed to be. He could hardly wait to get back to his tower up in the clouds.

But as he walked toward the tower, the voice seemed to get louder and louder. Every time he turned a corner, the voice seemed to draw closer. Finally, he heard the voice coming directly from behind a high hedge of thorn bushes.

"There is a child that needs help here!" he called out frantically. But none of the thirsty people in the dusty street so much as glanced at him.

There was nothing for the king to do but to help the child himself. As he fought through the hedge, a thorn pierced his right ear, and he felt a warm trickle of blood on his face. Finally, he broke through the hedge into a small courtyard. From a well in the center of the yard he heard a child's voice echoing, "Help!"

The king hurried to the well and looked down. He could see nothing. "Help me!" The king looked for a rope to lower into the well, but there was no rope. The only way to rescue the child was to descend into the pit himself. He might fall to his death, but he had no choice.

The king called down, "Don't worry. I am coming." Climbing over the side of the well and digging his fingers and toes into the cracks in the wall, he groped his way down into the darkness. As he lowered himself into the well, a sharp edge on the wall grazed his hand, cutting his right thumb. But he climbed on. His foot slipped and his right shoe went plunging to the bottom of the well. When he tried to find a toehold, his foot slipped again and the big toe on his right foot scraped against the rough wall. He could feel the blood soaking his silk stocking.

Still he struggled on, inch by inch, down, down into the well. It was dark as midnight around him. After what seemed like three hours, his feet finally rested on the dry floor of the well. He had no sooner stood up, relieved to be alive, when a child's arms grasped his leg with such force that he would have fallen over if the well had not been so narrow. It was a little boy. The king knelt before the boy and hugged him, while the grateful child wept on his shoulder.

"I was playing on the well," the boy whimpered. "And I slipped and fell."

"It is a miracle you are not dead," the king said.

"I thought I was," the boy answered. "It was so dark down here. And I thought no one would ever come to save me. Thank you. Thank you."

The king rested at the bottom of the well for a few moments. He hoped to rest longer, but suddenly the dry floor of the well became damp. Before long, a small puddle had formed. A minute later, the water was up to his ankles. "The well," the king said in amazement. "The water is flowing again. We have to get out before we drown."

The boy climbed onto the king's back, and together they began the long ascent from the pit. As the water churned and gurgled behind him, the king inched his way up the wall of the well. More than once, he thought the water was going to overwhelm him, but each time he pulled himself to safety. After what seemed like three days, the king pulled up out of the well. He and the boy fell to the ground, exhausted and grateful to be alive. A light warm rain was falling on the brown grass.

They lay on their backs as the rain pricked their faces. The rain became heavier and heavier. The king said, "We must find your home. Let me carry you." Shielding the boy with what was left of his robe, the king pushed his way back through the thorns into the street. He stood for a moment, his wet tattered robe flapping in the breeze, blood on his ear, thumb, and toe.

157

In the street, people were running this way and that, like ants do when you kick an anthill, which I am sure you have done at least once. Raindrops had gathered into puddles, and children danced and splashed, shrieking with joy. Across the street, someone saw the king, cried out, and pointed, and a great noisy crowd flooded toward him. Someone shouted, "Look, it is the widow's son! He is alive. The king has saved him."

A woman pushed her way through the crowd, and the boy in the king's arms reached to grasp her neck. "Mama!" he cried, as the weeping woman caught him.

"How can I ever thank you, O king," the widow said.

"What did you call me?"

"Are you not the king from the tower?" the widow asked, thinking she had made a mistake.

"Yes, but how did you know?"

"Because you saved my son," she replied. Then, looking at his tattered clothes and bloody face, hands, and feet, she added, "And because you look like a king."

Behind him, the king heard a shout. He turned and looked through the pathway he had made through the hedge of thorns into the courtyard. "The well's filled with water!" a man was shouting. "The springs are flowing again! We will have all the water we need!" Dozens of others, cups and buckets in hand, pressed through the narrow path to the well.

While the king watched in wonder, he felt a hand on his shoulder. He turned to see the wine seller balancing a barrel on his neck. The king ducked. "Naw. I'm not going to throw it at you. This is yours," he said. "Wine fit for a king greater than Caesar." There too was the baker, carrying the wedding cake. "Take it," he said. "I can make another for the wed-

ding. Food fit for a king greater than Charles." Finally came the jeweler, holding out the sparkling crown. "You should wear this crown. It fits you, I think. A crown for an emperor greater than Napoleon Bonaparte."

The king accepted the gifts gratefully. Then he called out, "This is a great occasion. The widow's son who was thought dead is alive. The drought is over. Let us celebrate. I will share my food and drink with you." The people of the city crowded into the town hall, where they ate wedding cake and drank lots and lots of wine. A few drank too much. It was almost morning by the time the last of the banqueters sloshed home through the flooded streets.

The next day, the king took his crown and returned to the tower that stretched above the clouds. Before he left, he announced that everyone in the city was welcome to come and go freely in his tower. Anyone who wished an audience with the king needed only to ask. And so the king ascended back into the clouds, content to know that, at least once in his life, he had truly acted like a king.

MORAL

A man's pride will bring him low,
but a humble spirit will obtain honor.
(Prov. 29:23)

Chapter XVIII

AN EXCELLENT WIFE

nd so Joseph became king when his father, King Lothar, died. The common people soon discovered that Joseph was a just ruler. Many who had thought Joseph would not make a good king had to admit that he was a better king than even his beloved father. Joseph spent his days sitting on his ivory throne at the gate of the capital city, settling quarrels among the people and passing sentences against criminals.

Many of the nobles, though, still thought one of his brothers would have been a better choice. The noble ladies hated and envied Queen Sophia. Joseph should have chosen a wife from a better family, they thought. Sophia was a mere shepherdess, and there were rumors her father was from another land.

But Sophia had little time to spend with such ladies. Most queens spend their time sitting around getting their portraits painted or watching jousts and pretending to be horrified by the sight of blood. Sophia was very different. Every morning, she got up before sunrise to light the lamps in every room of the palace, and every evening it was she who trimmed the wicks.

161

She helped prepare the king's food. Every morning and evening, she and the cooks roasted a lamb over the flames, made huge loaves of bread from fine flour and rich oil, and in the evening served the sweet blackberry wine in crystal chalices.

Between breakfast and dinner, while Joseph was busy with the work of a king, Sophia would go to the room that was used for spinning thread and making clothes. For many hours, she would spin at her wheel or weave at her loom or sew at her table. She made the most exquisite clothes in the kingdom. All her household, from Joseph to the least servant, wore scarlet, purple, and linen clothes that Sophia herself had made.

Once a week, Sophia would tour the gardens and examine the orchards and vineyards. Once, when she heard that a neighboring field was being sold, she went to the owner, offered a fair price, and so extended the boundaries of the royal gardens.

Joseph had been right. Sophia was the greatest gift a king could have. Joseph had made a wise choice.

"Next month I will have been king for seven years," Joseph said one evening as he and Sophia sat before a fire.

"And seven years since we married," Sophia replied as she gazed into the flames.

"I would like to hold a great feast to mark the occasion," Joseph continued. "We could invite all the most important people in the kingdom. It would last for a week, maybe two! It would be the greatest feast that ever was! Maybe we would have such a good time, the feast would go on forever and ever."

"I will prepare everything," Sophia said eagerly. Her mind was already full of ideas for food and drink and entertainment. Even if the feast did not last forever, she wanted it to be remembered to all eternity as a testimony to the greatness of her husband, good King Joseph.

Early the next morning, she began preparations. She told the royal butcher they would need seventy of the best bulls, fourteen of the healthiest rams, two hundred of the fattest lambs. She told the royal brewer that they would need a hundred barrels of beer and as many of wine. She told the royal baker they would need half a ton of the finest flour for pastries, cakes, breads, and rolls.

Sophia next visited the royal decorator. "The palace needs to be cleaned and prepared by the end of next month," she told him. "Polish the marble walls and mirrors, set precious stones in the walls all around. I want the whole palace to sparkle like a jewel."

Sophia decided she would personally invite the great nobles of the kingdom to the feast. After making sure her instructions were being followed, she set off with a dozen servants to invite the nobles.

They stopped that evening at the first of the great nobles' houses, where the lord invited them to stay for the night.

"It is a great honor," he said during dinner, "for the wife of the king to pay a visit to my home. Why have you honored me so?"

"I am traveling from the capital to the ends of the land with my twelve servants," Sophia said, "inviting the great nobles of the kingdom to a feast to celebrate King Joseph's seven years as king."

The nobleman swallowed hard. "Has it been that long?" he asked. Mumbling under his breath, he added, "Seems a lot longer to me."

163

Forcing a smile, he said, "Queen Sophia, I would very much like to come to your husband's great feast. Unfortunately, I cannot. You see, next month I will be traveling to visit some lands that I bought recently. I need to see if it is good farmland. I am sure you understand."

Sophia tried to smile but was greatly disappointed. "Yes, yes. I understand," she said softly.

The next morning, Sophia and her servants were off to the next great house. That evening, as they sat at dinner, Sophia invited the second nobleman to the feast.

At first, the nobleman frowned. Then his face brightened, and he answered, "Queen Sophia, there is nothing I would enjoy more than to attend the feast. But you see, I have recently bought some oxen to plow my fields, and I have not yet had a chance to use them. Next month, I will be very busy plowing with my new oxen. I am sure you understand."

"Yes, yes," Sophia answered. "I understand."

The next evening at dinner, Sophia invited the third nobleman to the feast.

"I will have to think about it," the third nobleman answered. "Perhaps I will tell you tomorrow evening, if you can stay, of course."

So, Sophia and her servants stayed until the evening of the second day. But at dinner on the second evening, the nobleman's answer was the same as it had been the first night. He asked Sophia to stay yet another night.

As they sat at the table on the third evening, Sophia once again invited the nobleman to the feast. "I would like to speak with you alone," the nobleman answered, motioning toward a doorway.

Sophia followed him down a high hallway into a dim room. The nobleman closed the door. "Queen Sophia, you are a very beautiful queen. I do not want you to be harmed. Please stay here in my house and be my wife."

"But I am already married to Joseph," Sophia cried.

"Ah, yes," the nobleman answered. "But if things go as planned, Joseph will not be king for long."

"What do you mean?" Despite her fright, Sophia was very angry.

"We great nobles have never liked your husband. He prefers the weak and helpless peasants and is always telling us how to treat our servants. We are planning to get rid of him—and soon! Stay with me and be my wife," the nobleman said, as he caught Sophia's arm.

"Never!" Sophia cried as she pulled away.

"As you wish," the nobleman said with mock politeness. "But perhaps you will change your mind in a week, when Joseph is no longer king. For the moment, you will stay here. I do not want you to rush home to warn your husband." With that, the nobleman turned and walked out, locking the door behind him.

The nobleman ordered that Sophia's twelve servants be taken into his dungeon and beaten without mercy. One servant, however, who had stayed in the barn to feed the horses, was able to escape without being detected, and so was able to warn Joseph about the plot.

Four days later, the silence of dawn was broken by the pounding of hoofs and the war cries of Joseph's soldiers. Eyes aflame, Joseph led the attack against the third nobleman's house, riding his white stallion, a blood-red cape streaming behind him. Joseph and his soldiers descended on the unprepared noble and brought that wretched noble and all his servants to a wretched end. Queen Sophia and her eleven servants were quickly released. From there, Joseph and his soldiers swept through the countryside, from one noble house to another, executing all the treacherous nobles who had plotted rebellion and burning their houses to the ground.

When they were both safely home in the palace and the land was again at rest, Sophia asked her husband, "Who will we invite to the feast? Only a few of the nobles were faithful to you and accepted your invitation."

Joseph thought a moment, then answered, "The nobles have had their chance, and they refused. They have received what they deserved. Now, go into the villages and highways, and invite whomever you find there to the feast. Invite the poorest of the poor, the lowest of the low. Tell them to bring their children and their parents and every last cousin. I want my feast to be full."

The next day, Sophia went out again with her servants, and invited the farmers and villagers, the shopkeepers and the beggars, the crippled, lame, and poor to the feast. All gladly accepted her invitation.

On the day of the feast, a throng of people too large to be numbered gathered at the doorway of the palace, pressing eagerly toward the door. Many were dressed in rough work clothes, some in rags.

When the palace servants saw them, they said, "Is the king going to let them into the palace dressed like that? Their clothes are dirty and plain."

Some in the crowd began to cry, while others turned to go. The servants were right. How could they attend the king's feast wearing rags? When Sophia heard it, she rushed to every closet in the palace and gathered all the fine clothes she could find. Then she went to meet the people at the door.

"Your clothes are filthy, it is true, and we cannot let you into the feast with such clothes. But do not cry and do not leave. There is good news. I have new clothes enough for all of you. Remove your filthy clothes, and put on these festive robes."

A cry of joy rose from the crowd. As each came to the door, his dirty clothes were removed and exchanged for clothes of scarlet and purple and linen. Then, dressed in new clothes, each crossed the threshold into the sparkling palace.

The feast was indeed the greatest feast that ever had been. Queen Sophia wore her white wedding dress that was covered with precious jewels. King Joseph was wrapped in a splendid robe of white. They sat enthroned together, eating and drinking. For seven days, the people ate meat and bread, drank wine and strong drink, and rejoiced with their sons and daughters in the presence of the king and his queen. When the week was over, King Joseph told them they could stay for yet another week to continue the feast. And so the feast went on and on, as Joseph had wished.

Toward the end of the feast, Joseph and Sophia rose from their thrones to dance. As they swept lightly across the floor of the great hall, the people stopped to watch in wonder. Dancing round and round the hall, the king and his bride melted together into a single blazing billow of light, and the whirling trains of their shimmering robes filled the whole palace.

MORAL

An excellent wife who can find?
For her worth is far above jewels.
(Prov. 31:10)

167

ABOUT The AUThOR

eter Leithart is a pastor in the Presbyterian Church in America and the author of *The Kingdom and the Power*. He and his wife, Noel, along with their seven children, currently reside in Cambridge, England where he is pursuing a doctorate in systematic theology. For several years prior to his studies in England, Mr. Leithart served as pastor of the Reformed Heritage Presbyterian Church (PCA) near Birmingham, Alabama. His graduate studies earned him the M.A.R. and the Th.M. degrees from Westminster Theological Seminary.